Born in Fez, Morocco, TAHAR BEN JELLOUN is an award-winning and internationally bestselling novelist, essayist, critic and poet. Regularly shortlisted for the Nobel Prize in Literature, he has won the Prix Goncourt and the International IMPAC Dublin Literary Award. His work has also been shortlisted for the Independent Foreign Fiction Prize. He received the rank of Officier de la Légion d'honneur in 2008. Some of his works in English translation include *The Happy Marriage*, *This Blinding Absence of Light*, *The Sand Child* and *Racism Explained to My Daughter*.

ROS SCHWARTZ has translated a wide range of Francophone fiction and non-fiction writers including Andrée Chedid, Aziz Chouaki, Fatou Diome, Dominique Manotti and Dominique Eddé. She was made Chevalier dans l'Ordre des Arts et des Lettres for her services to literature in 2009.

LULU NORMAN has translated the work of Mahi Binebine, Albert Cossery, Mahmoud Darwish, Amin Maalouf and the songs of Serge Gainsbourg. Her translations have been shortlisted for the International IMPAC Dublin Literary Award, Independent Foreign Fiction Prize and Best Translated Books Award, among others.

About My Mother

Tahar Ben Jelloun

Translated from the French by
Ros Schwartz and Lulu Norman

TELEGRAM

We dedicate this translation to Gary Pulsifer
– Ros Schwartz and Lulu Norman

Published 2016 in Great Britain by Telegram

First published as *Sur ma mère* by Editions Gallimard, France, 2008
Copyright © Tahar Ben Jelloun and Editions Gallimard 2008 and 2016

Translation © Ros Schwartz and Lulu Norman 2016

ISBN 978-1-84659-201-0
eISBN 978-1-84659-203-4

This book has been selected to receive English PEN's PEN Promotes and PEN
Translates Awards, supported by Bloomberg and Arts Council England as
part of the Writers in Translation programme. English PEN exists to promote
literature and its understanding, uphold writers' freedoms around the world,
campaign against the persecution and imprisonment of writers
for stating their views, and promote the friendly co-operation of
writers and free exchange of ideas.
www.englishpen.org

A full CIP record for this book is available from the British Library.

Printed and bound by CPI Group (UK) Ltd, Croydon, CR0 4YY

TELEGRAM
26 Westbourne Grove
London W2 5RH

www.telegrambooks.com

Supported using public funding by
**ARTS COUNCIL
ENGLAND**

1

Since she's been ill, my mother's become a frail little thing with a faltering memory. She summons members of her family who are long dead. She talks to them, is astonished that her mother hasn't come to visit, and sings the praises of her little brother who, she says, always brings her presents. They file past her bedside, sometimes they linger. I don't interrupt them, I don't like to upset her. Keltum, her paid companion, complains: 'She thinks we're in Fez, the year you were born!'

Mother's revisiting my childhood. Her memory's been toppled, lies scattered over the damp floor. Time and reality are out of kilter. She gets swept away by the emotions that come surging back. Every quarter of an hour, she asks me: 'How many children do you have?' Every time, I answer in the same even tone. Keltum is agitated and interrupts to say she can't stand Mother's repeated questions any more.

Mother's afraid of Keltum. She's a woman whose eyes betray her wicked thoughts and she knows it. When she speaks to me, she looks at the floor. When she greets me, she's obsequious, bowing and attempting to kiss my hand. I don't want to push her away, or put her in her place. I pretend not to know what she's up to. I can see fear in my mother's eyes. Fear that Keltum might leave her on her own when none of us are here. Fear that she won't give her her medication. Fear that she'll let her go without food, or worse, give her meat that's gone off. Fear that she might spank her, as if she were a naughty child. In one of her lucid moments, my mother said to me: 'I'm not mad, you know. Keltum thinks I'm a little girl again. She tells me off, she threatens me, but I know it's the pills playing tricks on me. Keltum's not a bad person, she's just prickly. She's tired. She's the one who washes me every morning, you know, son; she's the one who cleans up the stuff that leaks out of me. I couldn't ask that of you, or your brother, so Keltum's here for that too. It's as well to forget the rest …'

How can I forget that my mother's in the care of a woman who, over the years, has become hard, cynical and grasping? Why is my mother journeying back to childhood under the malevolent gaze of this bully?

Mother started talking about the midwife, Lalla Radhia, again. She insisted I invite her to lunch and told me where to go: 'She lives just before Batha, the big square at the entrance to the medina. Go to the café run by Sallam, Khaduj's husband – you know, Uncle Moulay Ali's daughter-in-law.

2

Go into the café and ask for her. Everyone knows her, she has to come!' I try to remind her that Lalla Radhia's no longer with us, but she insists she wants her at the house for lunch.

Since Mother's moved into a different bedroom, she's convinced she's in a different house and is living in a different city. We're no longer in Impasse Ali Bey in Tangier, but the Makhfiya district in Fez. We're no longer in the year 2000, but 1944. Her dreams won't be extinguished. They assail her waking hours, refuse to leave her alone. The present is lurching. It flickers, sputters back to life and then fades altogether. It no longer concerns her. She's become detached from it, which doesn't worry her in the least.

She tells me she saw a man and a woman talking in the hallway. They must have come to buy the old house in Fez. She warns me not to let it go cheaply: 'Times are hard. The war's not over and besides, your father won't be happy! I heard the man say to the woman, "It's a bargain, we should seize the opportunity." Anyone would think they lived with us and knew we were struggling. The man's not from Fez, he has a country accent – Fassi's more refined. And in any case, we're not selling!'

Today, Zineb, her nurse, has come to change her dressings. No longer able to recognise her, Mother refuses to let her touch her foot. Zineb says she won't hurt her. Mother smiles: 'If you do, my father will know all about it. I'm not a child, so go on, clean the wound and don't treat me like a frightened little girl.' Then things fall back into place and she remembers everything. It was just a lapse. A memory lapse. Her recollections are a little hazy.

Mother threw a pretty gold chain down the toilet. Keltum fished it out and washed it repeatedly for two days, then soaked it in adulterated eau de cologne.

My sister has come from Fez to look after her. Mother's annoyed: she thinks she's her own mother. My sister's getting on a bit too, she's only sixteen years younger than my mother, the daughter of her first marriage. Mother remembers very clearly: 'I'd just turned fifteen. My husband was strong and handsome. The typhus epidemic carried him off before my daughter was born. A widow at sixteen!'

2

There were foreigners in town but it wasn't yet wartime. I think I'd been noticed at the hammam; that was often where mothers chose wives for their sons. I remember, an older lady came over to my mother and asked her for a little rasul: 'Mine's finished. But our sort can help each other out, can't we, Lalla Hajjah?' My mother, who hadn't yet made the pilgrimage, answered: 'God has not yet shown me the way to Mecca, I wait and I hope – but here, take this rasul, it's from Chrif Wazzani's. It smells lovely and it's good for the skin.' I listened to this exchange, little suspecting it was a marriage proposal. True, at one point the lady murmured in my mother's ear: 'May God protect your gazelle, whose skin is so white and whose hair is so long!' That's what people say when they want to propose marriage: 'May God protect her and keep her from wicked people's eyes!'

A few days later, sounding half-hearted, even resigned, my mother said: 'I think, daughter, you're about to be married. Your father consents, especially since he knows the family of the young man whose mother I met. They're a Chorfa *family, noble people, descendants of our beloved Prophet. The young man works with his father, who's a trader in the Diwane, right beside your uncle Sidi Abdesslam – as a matter of fact, he was the one who thought of you when he saw how well the young man was doing. The mother seems a good person from a fine family; we found out that our parents knew each other well. They're a true Fassi family like us, and you know, daughter, a Fassi girl can only be happy with a Fassi man of her class. Our kind don't mix, our forebears knew that only too well and cultivated relationships within the same prominent family. I'd never give my daughter to a man whose family wasn't known to us, someone from another city like Casablanca or even Meknès. A Fassi man for a Fassi woman, that's a guarantee and a precautionary measure we shouldn't ignore.'*

I listened to her, not saying a word. I was intrigued, and afraid: 'But Yemma, I'm barely fifteen! I still play with dolls.'

'Daughter, did you know that the last wife of our beloved Prophet – his favourite, Aisha – was only twelve when he married her? You're the daughter of a man as important and respected as a saint. You're the daughter of a Cherif, *a descendant of the Prophet. I myself was given to your father by my parents when I was sixteen.'*

'How old is he, this boy from a good family?'

6

'Are you crazy? Your uncle Sidi Abdesslam spoke so highly of him to your father that we wouldn't dream of questioning his judgement. All I know is that he's a fine young man, from an excellent family, well known to us, and that he works with his father in the Diwane. That's it, you'll find out more on your wedding night, just as I did. Do you imagine I'd seen your father before the wedding? It was a mutual discovering, and I've been the happiest woman in the world.'

'So he must be young!'

'Oh yes! It's his first marriage; he's not one of those old men looking for a second or third wife.'

'Yemma, I'll never go against your wishes, I'll do everything you tell me to as long as I have your blessing.'

'Since I want only what's best for you, you have nothing to fear! You know, daughter, my heart is a little heavy. Every marriage is a gamble, you never know how things will turn out, which is why we find out about the family, about their background – that's very important, because it gives us some idea of the boy's upbringing. The problem arises where there is dishonesty. That happened with my cousin Sidi Larbi, who was saddled with the elder sister of the girl his mother had asked for as a wife. How could he know? He only found out on the wedding night – as did we, by the way – but since our tradition does not permit divorce, he stayed married to her. She's a good person, not beautiful at all, but sweet-natured. Still, you have nothing to fear, Sidi Drissi is a fine young man, we know the entire family well.'

7

3

My mother's body continues to shrink. She is tiny. A tiny, light little thing with meagre flesh that causes her pain. Her sight has deteriorated but her hearing is perfect. She detected the call to prayer in the chirping of a sparrow. She said: 'It's calling God.' My sister didn't contradict her; she agreed the bird was an angel come to pray with them.

Once again she confused me with my older brother, asking me how his children were, getting everything muddled. Then she thought my children were my brother's. I prefer to see the funny side, but he gets upset and his eyes fill with tears. I feel like crying too, but resist, because at times she is perfectly lucid and I see her as she always was – beautiful and graceful, clever and astute, conscious of what she's suffering and of everything going on around her. She never loses her mind completely. My brother took it upon himself to work out how long her moments of clarity last compared with her rambling. He claims the periods when her mind wanders last longer.

Yesterday, sounding embarrassed, Keltum asked me to buy some pads. Mother's increasingly incontinent, but she refuses to wear them. She tears off the adhesive strips and flings the pads under the bed. Keltum's furious. She can't take it any more: 'You're only here a few hours, but for me it's all the time, day and night – and it's worse at night. She hardly sleeps and wakes us up to talk about Fez and her brothers, who died a long time ago. Tell the doctor to give her a pill that will give her back her mind, or make her sleep. I can't stand this any longer!'

Mother's always had a serene attitude towards death. Her faith in God has driven out any fear of it. Once, in the days when her health gave no cause for alarm, she asked me for a large sum of money. 'Why? Don't be like your father, always asking what I wanted money for. I'm going to redo the sitting room, buy some new fabric, repaint the entire house, get two lovely low tables and some more cutlery and napkins.' And why all that? 'I want the house to be clean and tidy for my funeral. People will come from all over the country: I want them to find the house looking nice. They must be served good food; I've always received my guests generously. My farewell should be lavish, the best reception of all! That's why I need money, son. I'm telling you now, and don't forget. It has to be a grand occasion.'

My friend Roland's mother celebrated her ninetieth birthday by going round the world. She lives in Lausanne, and her health is good, she plays bridge every day, reads books and goes to the cinema. Life in Switzerland is less tiring than it is in Fez. My mother never went to school, she doesn't know how to play bridge, has never been to the theatre or the opera. She's had three husbands and given birth to four children, fed them and raised them. Three husbands and only one true love. I've never heard her tell the story – I guessed. My mother doesn't talk about love. It's a word she uses only for her children. She says: 'I'd die for you, light of my eyes, rainbow of my life, I'd die for you!' She's uneducated but not uncultured, she has her own culture, religious beliefs, values and traditions. To live an entire life without ever deciphering a page of writing, without ever being able to read numbers, to live in a closed world surrounded by signs, unable to understand them … The problem became acute the day my father had the telephone installed: she felt the need to learn numbers so she could call her children, her sister and her husband. My father taught them to her but soon lost patience, leaving her with the numbers written large on a slate. She decided to learn two phone numbers, no more: mine and the one for my father's shop. She spent all day dialling them until she'd learned them by heart. One day she managed to dial mine correctly but to her disappointment she got the answerphone. She spoke to it: 'You, machine, you're the machine of my son in lafrance, aren't you? Now you listen to me, and whatever you do, make sure you don't forget a word I say, so you can tell him when he gets back. Now you tell him that his mother called, she's fine – well, more or less, she's dying to see him. Tell him too that his father's coughing a lot and won't go to the doctor. You must make a point of that, so he'll call his doctor friend and get him to come over. He's coughing up and spitting out nasty stuff. Tell him too that his sister Touria has gone to Mecca. So that's it, machine, don't forget to tell him to speak to his father, tell him as well that my blood sugar's up after Keltum upset me. Right, I'm putting the phone down and I'm counting on you to pass on the message. One more thing – I'll be quick – tell him that El Haj, his cousin, has lost his wife and he should call to offer his condolences. Thank you, thank you very much!'

4

My mother has worked all her life – in the kitchen, and keeping house. It hasn't been easy for her. I remember her irritation when the primus stove was blocked and she had to delicately remove the gunge that had collected in the rising tube. I remember life with no refrigerator, with no gas stove, no running water, no telephone. My mother wore herself out. The servants she hired took advantage of her weakness. How many times did she find herself cooking lunch for fifteen people, on her own – last-minute guests, family members who'd arrived unexpectedly? They'd often come to spend holidays at our house.

She had to be nice to them, smile and come out with all the traditional platitudes: 'Today's a very special day. You light up our house, you fill it with your goodness, may God give life to those who behold you. Please bear with us, accept us as we are, we haven't adequately prepared for your visit. Forgive us, this is a special day, a very special day,' and so on.

She'd trot out the words, thinking of the huge amount of work this impromptu visit would entail. She had no choice, what could she do? Those who come to your house require your protection, your hospitality. Sometimes they'd be members of her husband's family and she'd welcome them with the same warmth, the same smile as if they were her own relatives. She'd overdo things because she couldn't bear the slightest criticism from her husband or from her mother-in-law. It was a question of dignity.

She knew she was being tested. How does the new little bride receive guests? We'll find out straight away, we'll turn up at her home without warning …

She'd be riddled with anxiety that she wasn't up to the mark. Mother enjoyed entertaining but not when she was unprepared. A stickler for rules and traditions, she was afraid that she wouldn't have enough food, she'd be shamed. Even yesterday, she made me reiterate my promise to arrange a sumptuous funeral for her: 'If you take care of it, I know you'll do things properly, make it a real occasion. You are generous and I love you for that, I always have. You've always had a special place deep in my heart. You have to promise me, so I can depart with one less thing to worry about!'

Yesterday was one of her lucid days. She went over all the things she'd said that hadn't made sense: 'Do you know, son, I thought your father was still alive and I couldn't understand why he hadn't come to see me. Oh, my mind can't keep hold of anything nowadays, it keeps playing tricks on me and I feel so ashamed. I know your father died ten years ago. I know your cousin's wife died in childbirth thirty years ago. All these dead people flitting around in my head! It must be the diabetes, it must be all the pills I've been taking for such a long time …

'Anyway, I feel good today, everything's clear, I know what's going on. But tell me, you're not going to sell this house, are you? I like it here, I prefer it to the house we had last year, the one by the sea.' I correct her: 'No, Yemma, the house by the sea was thirty years ago. Here, where you live, this isn't a new house.'

'And this garden: our house didn't have a garden …'

All this because she's moved to a different room. From her window she can see an ancient fig tree and a few plants. Before, she lived in the sitting room that gives onto the tiny garden. The door and windows didn't close properly. It was draughty. The doctor made her change rooms.

My mother cried this morning. She says her children have been taken away from her, that they were wrenched from her while she was nursing them. She always had beautiful breasts and very soft skin. 'I had one baby on my right breast, another on my left. I was feeding them. They were very hungry. Then a woman dressed in black from head to toe rushed over and pulled them off me. I felt pain right at the root of my breasts, a knife slicing into my flesh. Then the

14

babies went up to heaven; suddenly they were gone. I'll have to go and look for them.'

Mother's always been small. My father used to laugh at her. She'd take it badly. One day he called her '*media mujer*' (half a woman). That made her laugh. These days she doesn't talk about being short. She talks about her worries, her obsessive attachment to certain objects: her plastic prayer beads brought back from Mecca by one of her daughters-in-law, her glasses, the polished stone for doing her ablutions, her purse in which she keeps a few notes … Keltum must have taken advantage of her memory lapses more than once to extract money from her. Mother's not in charge of the housekeeping money any more. I don't know whether Keltum steals because she has an increasing need for money or because it's a compulsion, a kind of illness. Mother's often complained she's been robbed. She says: 'But I turn a blind eye, it doesn't matter, as long as they leave my children alone … Money's nothing, it's the dirt of life.'

My mother's never known how to conduct herself with the women who worked in her house. She quickly became very close to them, treated them like family. Then she couldn't understand why they left her, taking valuable items with them: 'I treated them like my own – I shared my meals with them, I gave them presents, even some of my dresses, and in return, they cheated me, abandoned me … Country people and mountain people are jealous of city folk, it's no wonder they lose their heads and begin to steal …'

Last year, alerted by our doctor, my aunt came hurrying over to see her. It was a false alarm. My mother detected something like disappointment on her sister's face. She thought she could read her mind: 'I came rushing over, only to find my sister fit as a fiddle. What a waste of my time!' She didn't say anything, but the visit was a brief one.

It reminds me of Ozu's film, *Tokyo Story*. One of the sons, who's raced to his father's bedside, regrets having made an unnecessary journey and says: 'If he were to die now, that would be quite convenient for my wife and me, it would save us making the journey again!' When I'm with my family, I sometimes feel as if I'm in an Ozu film. I see them all in black and white. I turn down the sound and close my eyes. For years, my mother's sister has chosen to make light of things. She likes to joke, and sometimes says hurtful things. Life has been kind to her – she married a rich, very sophisticated man who refused her nothing. Sometimes she'd taunt my mother, criticising her for not travelling abroad, for not demanding her husband give her fine things. Mother couldn't remind her that we were poor, that we couldn't afford to live as she did.

All her life, Mother's been haunted by the fear of losing her house, of finding herself shunted from one city to another, a burden to her sons, the last straw for her daughters-in-law, yet another worry for her daughter who'd suffered from chronic depression since losing her husband. She remembered her own mother's final years, when she'd lived with one of her sons, who died prematurely, so then she was taken in by her daughter. She'd lost her 'place', her dignity: no longer in her own home, she stayed in other people's. It wasn't the same, no matter how kind they were.

She saw her mother weeping and complaining that she wasn't getting any attention, she was taken for granted, she suffered from loneliness and a lack of consideration. She was oversensitive. Which wasn't surprising in a very elderly, obsessive woman, nostalgic for the days when she'd lived like a queen.

5

This morning, she's looking for her very fine, gold-embroidered *cherbil*, the pretty *babouche* slippers worn by young brides. 'Where have my *cherbil* gone, my beautiful golden *cherbil*, embroidered all over by the hand of Moishe, the rabbi's son, the great expert in gold thread? My *cherbil*, it must be Keltum that's stolen them from me, she steals and then hides the things she takes under the bed. As soon as I close my eyes, she calls her children or her grandchildren and gives them the things she's collected to take home. My *cherbil*, my beautiful *cherbil* ...'

The drawing up of the marriage certificate takes place on a Friday, after the midday prayer. Two aduls *come in, wearing white djellabas, red felt tarbouches – the nationalists' emblem – and delicate yellow* babouches. *They are followed by the male relatives of the bridegroom and the men from my mother's family. It's a gathering of men; the women remain hidden from view in adjoining rooms. They watch the ceremony from behind the curtain, peeping discreetly through a chink. The certificate is drawn up in silence. Bride and groom are asked to give their full names and dates of birth. They give the approximate year. This is Fez, in 1936. Moroccans do not have public records. People know each other and have no need to check birth dates. They say: 'He was born the year of the great drought,' or 'It must have been when the French had just arrived in Morocco,' 'He was born the same year as the Sultan's son, do you remember?' 'It was springtime ...' Or again, without naming my mother, they said: 'Moulay Ahmed's daughter was born the year it snowed in Fez,' then they'd talk about that rare event. People had never seen snow, so white, so strange. They slithered about, fell over and then struggled to stand up again, laughing. Then, one morning, the snow vanished – not completely – it melted into the mud and turned to slush. 'Yes, I remember,' says Moulay Ahmed. 'We were very cold, we weren't used to snow. That was the day my daughter – God keep and protect her – came into the world. God chose that day to bring light to my home.' Then they turn to the bridegroom's father. He hesitates, and then says: 'My son – may God make him a man, a true man – was born the day the kissaria went on strike. The Christians moved in and no one wanted them. So it must have been 1916 – that's right, twenty years ago.'*

'By the grace of the Almighty, Sidi Abdesslam Al Idrissi, on behalf of his son Mohammed – may God protect him and

keep him on the straight and narrow path – has taken a wife, Lalla Fatma, daughter of Moulay Ahmed and under her father's protection, a virgin of marrying age. And with her is offered a blessed dowry amounting to a total of 20,000 rials. The bride's father has received the agreed sum from the hands of the above-named bridegroom's father, as witnessed by the two notaries undersigned.

'This marriage takes place under the most auspicious circumstances, as prescribed by Muslim law, governed by the precepts of the Qur'an, which commands that the husband act with kindness, fairness and consideration towards his wife, or otherwise restores her freedom, in accordance with due procedure.

'The bride's father has given his daughter in marriage by virtue of the power vested in him by God. The groom agrees wholeheartedly to this act concluded on his behalf by his father; he ratifies and is bound by it.

'May Almighty God bless this union and assist in the accomplishment of His plans. May God show them the path of happiness, trust, kindness and mutual support.'

The men rise. The elder adul stands between the two fathers and begins the 'Fatiha', his hands together pointing up to God, and they pray.

'Let us now pray for goodness, for the couple's happiness, that Allah will show them the path to goodness, that Allah will instil in them high morals and, with the blessing of their parents, that Allah will show them the great paths of life. May He give them children to make their family grow and fill their house, which is so beautiful and so welcoming. May Allah keep them in His goodness and in our religion's faith, in His mercy and tolerance! Amen, Amen!'

They draw their hands across their lips, then over their hearts, while continuing to chant prayers: 'Glory to God, God Almighty, Lord of the universe!'

They congratulate one another, saying: 'Blessed and happy be this union! May God make this union succeed! May it prove lasting, in goodness, joy and kindness!'

'Now,' says the elder adul, 'these children are married according to the rites of our religion, the sadaqah has been given to the bride's family, the marriage will be consummated when the two families have agreed a date, and when the bride's family has her trousseau and her house ready.'

6

For the past two days, my mother's been asking for someone called Mustafa. We don't have a Mustafa in the family. Who is she talking about? She persists, saying she's annoyed that he's not here. When we ask her who she means, she's surprised we're asking such a silly question. 'But he's my eldest son, the one I had when I was fifteen, how can you not remember him? He's a handsome, generous man. He has several children, I can't remember how many. His wife has him well trained, he doesn't do a thing without asking her first, or rather he only does what she orders him to. Mustafa has a heart of gold, a heart as pure as silk. I'm sure it's his wife who's stopping him coming to visit me. If you see him, tell him his mother says he must come.'

There's no one with that name in our family. Where did she get this idea – could it be a son she's never spoken about before? Is she confusing him with my older brother?

According to Keltum, my mother cried all night. In the morning, she couldn't remember a thing. She was crying because she believed the courts had taken away her two very young children. 'What am I supposed to say to that?' Keltum asks me. There's nothing you can say. You just have to listen and not contradict her.

Yesterday, Mother asked me for money. Not much, just so she wouldn't feel completely penniless. Keltum manages the housekeeping now. I give my mother a 100-dirham note. She tries to cram it into her pocket, which is full of rags. She's afraid she'll run out of handkerchiefs. A little later, she asks in the same tone for some money. She's already forgotten. When I remind her I've already given her 100 dirhams, she replies: 'Keltum stole it from me.' Then, after a while, she looks at me, stares hard and says: 'Who are you, monsieur? You know my brother, the one whose wife made a doormat of him? He's so sweet, he doesn't dare go against the woman he calls Lalla Lallati ... Listen, I have to go, Mother's taking me to see Moishe, who's doing the embroidery for my trousseau. He's the best in the whole *mellah*, he has golden fingers. He's so good, he's practically a Muslim!'

What's this disease called? Alzheimer's? There are times when Mother's perfectly lucid and coherent. Granted, these moments are increasingly rare. What does it matter what name is given to this illness? What's the point of naming it? She says: 'My memory's getting blurry. As I get older, my mind's shrinking: it can't keep hold of everything, there

23

are too many things. Ask me some questions, just to see if it's all still there.' She recites the names of her children and grandchildren, mixes up times and cities, corrects herself, laughs at her decrepitude and protests because her favourite singers aren't on Moroccan TV these days.

She who's never missed a prayer doesn't pray any more. She no longer remembers how to do her ablutions with the polished stone or what to say in her prayers. Keltum tells me: 'She soils herself and knows that being unclean, she can't pray.'

My mother's become very impatient. When she asks for something, she shouts and complains. Keltum's impatient too. Caring twenty-four hours a day for an elderly person who's lost their mind requires more than patience. Sometimes she loses her temper and demands a holiday – another way of asking for a raise – and I don't argue. Her work has no price. Taking a frail, elderly woman in your arms, carrying her to the bathroom to wash her, dressing and comforting her, answering the same question for the tenth time, taking her back to her room, giving her her medication, cooking her meals, talking to her, never leaving her. Only her own daughter could have done that, but my sister Touria suffers from depression and has no patience with her mother.

Mother's agreed to go for a drive outside the city. Ahmed, who used to work in Father's shop, has lent me his Mercedes, which is more comfortable than my Fiat Uno. We carry her to the car, settle her in and adjust her glasses. She's happy and excited. She prays that all will go well. We reverse out and

24

she wonders what's happening to her. She doesn't recognise the little street or the neighbours. Her friend, who used to live opposite, has moved away. She reminisces about the afternoons they used to spend together. I drive slowly so she can take in the scenery. I drive up to Cap Spartel, stop near the lighthouse and explain to her that this is where two seas meet, the Atlantic and the Mediterranean. She listens but looks thoughtful. She tells me where her son Mohammed's house is. I remind her that he lives in Casablanca. 'He might have told me,' she mutters. I don't argue with her. We continue our drive as far as the Mirage, a lovely hotel overlooking the sea. At first, she refuses to get out of the car, she's afraid of being seen in this condition. We sit her in a chair and Ahmed and I carry her into the shade of a tree, facing the swimming pool. She says: 'Is it yours, all this? Is this your villa? You deserve it. It's beautiful – the swimming pool, the sea, the grass, all this green, and the silence! You've chosen a fine spot, may God grant you even more good luck and kindness so that you and your family live long lives, with no misfortune!' I explain that it's a hotel where I often come for the summer. She says: 'This place is like you, it's beautiful.' Then she dozes, wakes with a start and asks for Keltum: 'Get all the things for the baths, we're going to the hammam, I'm going to be married tomorrow, hurry up, we mustn't be late. Mother's very busy, all my cousins are here for the hamman ceremony, I'm to be married tomorrow. I'm scared, I haven't met my husband, I don't know if he's tall and handsome or short and ugly. I don't know if he has all his teeth, or if he'll like me. Let's get the hammam things ready. Don't forget the oranges and the hard-boiled eggs, don't forget the scented *rasul* and the Moulay Idriss henna. Hurry, girls, hurry, or the light will be gone.'

7

All the female cousins of her age are here, laughing and joking, proud to accompany the youngest of them to the hammam ceremony. They each have a brass bowl. There are around ten of them. Ambar, the black girl who used to be Moulay Ahmed's slave, takes charge: 'Follow me, gather round our princess, our beauty, the gazelle who tomorrow will be given to a good man, a man from a fine family, the man who'll make her happy and give her children. May God bless them and bring them joy.'

The entire hammam has been hired for the occasion. Zubida, the attendant, greets the procession with a string of ululations. Ambar calls on the Prophet and his companions. The women who will wash and massage their bodies – the tayabates – are waiting. The cousins undress, leaving their clothes at the entrance, next to suitcases containing new outfits, and enter the hammam squealing with joy. The cousins tease Ambar, whose enormous breasts make them laugh. She's fat *but she doesn't care. Her breasts hang like heavy fruit. The girls are proud of their firm little busts. They touch and tickle one another, giggling, slithering around and almost falling over. A masseuse takes the bride-to-be in hand. She strokes her slowly, washes her, and then begins to give her a thorough massage. After a while, feeling tired, Ambar asks if they can rest for a moment, just to eat a few oranges. They move from the steam room to the warm room. Here, they can breathe. They eat, drink cool water and relax, then go back to the steam room to finish cleansing their skin. The masseuse shows them how to scrub away the dead skin painlessly. She tells them: 'This is the cemetery of useless skin.' It's also the place where everything superfluous is removed. Hair – oh, hair must be removed. When the husband goes to bed with his gazelle, he must encounter only softness, a smooth skin, velvety and beautiful – everything that he is not. 'You see, girls, a woman's skin must be pampered, her entire body must be prepared. Her mind too must be readied, but on the wedding night, it's her body that's being tested. A word of advice for our lovely gazelle who'll be given to her husband tomorrow: slide through his hands like a fish, don't give yourself to him straight away, make him chase you a little, let him win you. You smell good, you're ready, there isn't a hair on your entire body. You're a ripe fruit, but he has to make some effort. Be obedient, of course, but you're also allowed to play a little. After all, you're still a child, a girl of barely fifteen!'*

Now comes the taqbib: *the* tayabates *have filled seven buckets with water, some hot, some warm. They dip their* bowls into them and pour the water over the head of the bride-to-be. They claim that the bowls they use for scooping the water come from Mecca. After the seven dousings, they announce that the gazelle is under the protection of the angels.

Three hours later, Ambar notices that the gazelle can't take any more, she's fainting. Ambar picks her up and carries her to the room where the steam is bearable. She wraps her in a big fouta – a bath towel bought for the occasion – and takes her to the resting room. She gives her a glass of milk, then makes her inhale a strong perfume. The girls join her. To comfort her, cousin Aisha says whatever comes into her head: 'It's all the emotion, the fateful day is getting closer. You're so lucky, when will it be my turn? I'm too old, almost twenty and still not wed. I'm the eldest and my younger sister was married before me, the world's upside down. But I'm pretty – not as pretty as you are, but I can wait. What's been written for me will come to pass … I won't end up on the shelf …'

8

My friend Dr Fattah made me a promise: if Mother's health suddenly deteriorates, he has a duty to let me know. He calls me in May. I can tell it's serious from the tone of his voice: he speaks gently, weighs his words and simply says what needs saying. The next day I'm at her bedside. I see she's in the room where my father died, ten years earlier. My first impression is the worst: the colour of her skin, pale and jaundiced, her glassy eyes staring at the ceiling, her lower jaw contorted and sucked in, mouth wide open, gaze vacant. My mother, visited by death. With tears in his eyes, my brother says: 'I've arranged to see El Haj, our cousin. He knows what arrangements we need to make for the grave and the funeral: her condition is hopeless.'

Despite what I see, despite the doctors' very guarded prognoses, my intuition tells me otherwise. My mother isn't about to die. Not this time. She doesn't know where she is or who is around her. I take her hand and speak to her softly. Close family members come and go. In her rare lucid moments, she gives orders to Keltum to start cooking dinner and laying the table, insisting the tablecloths be clean and ironed. We take turns at her bedside, but my sister and Keltum never leave her.

How to pass the time at my mother's bedside? Once the high emotion has subsided, you begin to get bored. There's nothing to do. You greet visitors, you answer the phone, you keep an eye on her breathing. You wait for the doctors to come, you stare at the walls, following the lines of cracks caused by damp. You gaze at the ceiling. You do nothing. You wait, you chat to the nurses. I've learned things about this private hospital. Not so nice, some of the things that go on here. Money makes people crazy. Some nurses are paid 1,000 dirhams a month, others aren't paid at all because they're considered trainees. Public hospitals aren't much better. I prefer a well-equipped, efficient hospital to a Parliament where people spend hours pontificating. But that's another story. It all went well for my mother, this time. We paid in advance, slipped some fat tips to the nursing staff. The doctors were competent.

When she left the hospital, she had no idea what had happened. There was no problem taking her home. She thought she'd just moved to a different bedroom and then a different house. She had no recollection of her stay in the hospital. Just as well. My mother's dearest wish can be summed up by this prayer: 'May God let me die in your lifetime!' She is distraught at the thought of losing a child, as any mother would be. She saw how her own mother had suffered when one of her sons died prematurely. A fathomless grief. Something she daren't even imagine – it is too painful. 'I'll die, yes, but with my children all around me.'

I've come to understand that demand: it stems from her all-consuming love. What do you do with that love if one of your children is carried off by a brutal death – called back to God, as she says? Muslim mystics, the Sufis, talk about God's love in very similar terms. My mother was no mystic but she celebrated the simple things and essential values. She did this by giving of herself, without making an issue of it or suffocating her children. One day, during a radio broadcast, I said that my Muslim mother was a 'Jewish mother' and I added, 'a Jewish mother who doesn't smother'. She'd say to us: 'I'd die for you: my heart never gives up, it keeps me going. Whenever I'm worried about you, my heart pounds, my love chokes me. That's just how I am: there's nothing to be done, I can't help it. You can laugh, but when you have children of your own, you'll understand the kind of worry that burns in your chest. I'm always thinking about you, and I'm scared by the way people look at you. The evil eye is real, you know, and frighteningly powerful, it reaches everywhere like an octopus, seeking out happiness to destroy. There are people who want to hurt you just because you have your health, because you exist. God keep you safe from people's evil looks! May He protect you from their venom! May God lift you above their cruelty and make you a light to guide those who live in the dark! The human heart isn't always kind. But it's not in my nature to be suspicious. I believe what I'm told. I trust that people are sincere and act in good faith, but I just cannot lie and pretend. That's why I get hurt, but I'd rather be as I am. It's the way I was brought up. My mother was the same. My father was a saint; people came to him for advice. He was known for his kindness and his learning. I inherited that goodness from him but sometimes it doesn't do me any favours. But no matter! I have you and that's what counts ... That's why I ask God in His mercy to let me go, surrounded by all of you. We'll pray together and I'll go gently, like my mother.'

My mother's youngest sister is an energetic woman who enjoys life. She married a man from a wealthy family. That family made a deep impression on us, growing up in Fez. They were the first to buy a motor car, to have a house in the country (where we were invited to stay in the spring), to have a telephone and, most importantly, the first Fassi family to move out of the medina. They were rich people who loved the simple things in life, even though they put on a faintly superior air, to remind us that we didn't belong to the same class. But they never managed to make my mother feel inferior. Nor my father, who'd criticise their way of life, which made them laugh. My father had a tremendous sense of humour and took great pleasure in his use of irony. My aunt would tease him, and he in turn made fun of her 'lifestyle' and her preoccupation with appearances over more fundamental things. People said that his words mixed salt and sugar, honey and pepper, cruelty and raw truth. He wasn't afraid to say things that were hurtful, but true.

My aunt came to see my mother. She always brought a salutary dose of cheer. She was shocked when Mother took her for someone else, saying: 'My sweet darling, I've been waiting for you such a long time.' And then she confused her daughter with her mother again. Addressing her sister, she said: 'You know, darling, my mother's here – yes, your grandmother – she's here but she doesn't recognise me. That's not nice of her. She came from Fez and all she can think about is when she's leaving again. I've done nothing to hurt her. Speak to her, she'll listen to you. Ask her why Amina hasn't come. It's not like her; she's always rushed to my bedside. I'm her older sister, I brought her up, along with my daughter, I think they even nursed at the same breast. I was young and healthy. My mother wasn't strong enough to look after the house and all her children, so she asked me to look after Amina, and I treated her like my own daughter. They're the same age. Work it out, you'll see they were born the same year, just six months apart.'

Mother's sitting on the edge of her bed. Her left foot's more swollen than her right, the dressing must be a little tight. As usual, she's wearing a pink *tchamir*, a kind of long robe, and a white headscarf. Since her hair's turned white, she's been covering her head. She's wearing a gold bracelet. Mother is bored. She looks at the window and says nothing, shifts her position, places her bad foot on the bed and stares at the wardrobe opposite. She calls for Keltum, who doesn't answer straight away. She calls her again. Keltum shouts: 'I'm coming.' 'Hurry up,' says my mother. Keltum arrives, looks as if she's about to shout at her, then says: 'Only God can put up with her.' My mother cries: 'Don't leave me alone! Why do you shut yourself away on the other side of the house and abandon me? I'm going to tell God in my prayers and you'll see, my saintly father won't like it. Come over here, sit down and don't move!'

Mother and Keltum are bored. They both stare intently at a corner of the room. On TV there's an American soap opera dubbed into Spanish. The colours are garish. The images fall from the screen and mingle with the dust on the carpet. My mother smiles, she's all alone. Keltum dozes. The phone rings. Highlight of the day. 'It's your son calling.' 'Which one?' 'The one who phones every day!'

I speak to my mother. When I ask 'How are you?' I always get the same response: 'I'm here, picking up a few crumbs of time until God decides to release me. I'm in His hands. Death is certain; there's no point talking about it. I'm just waiting!' I ask Keltum how things are. She owes me the truth; she tells me whether my mother's slept well, or if she has diarrhoea or has been hallucinating. I speak to my mother again and she complains about Keltum, laughing. When she laughs, it's a good sign. Then I ask for her prayers and her blessing. She knows them by heart and puts all her energy into them, with no mistakes or hesitation. When she blesses me, my mother is fully there. She raises her eyes to the heavens and

35

addresses God. Just listening to her makes me feel protected. It's not rational, but I don't question it. My mother sees me as a fragile creature whose way needs lighting. She's forever praying that I'll be kept safe from enemies, from bad, jealous people. She sees them and chases them away with her hand.

For a long time now, my mother has prayed sitting down, with her eyes closed. She murmurs her prayers, wiggles her right index finger and concludes by joining her hands, pointing them upwards and telling God her dearest wishes.

These days she talks of nothing but her jewellery. She says it's all disappeared. She shared it out among her granddaughters and daughters-in-law a few years ago, saying: 'I'd rather give you my jewellery now, so there'll be no arguing after I die, I'm just keeping this bangle and this necklace.' That was the necklace she'd thrown down the toilet. Keltum thought it was hers by rights. My mother claimed it. Keltum flung it onto the bed, saying: 'I should have left it in her shit.' The bangle, impossible to get off her wrist now, was safe.

9

That necklace is precious. My mother wore it on her wedding night. It was a long night, an interminable night. Adorned with jewellery, she waited, surrounded by negafates *– women companions whose job was to ensure the ceremony was conducted properly. The celebrations took place in two houses. The girl's family waited while the bridegroom's kinsmen readied themselves to come and take the bride away. Time dragged on. The girl was drowsy, she could hardly keep her eyes open. Tiredness from the hammam and the tension of the day heightened her fear and sharpened her curiosity about the man who was to be her husband for life. Because in those families, divorce did not exist. Marriage was for ever, whether you were happy or not.*

The girl waits and counts her years, her months. She re-counts several times. Fifteen years and seven months, or sixteen years and a few weeks? She had been told she was five years older than her brother, that her little sister was still a baby: 'So that makes me fifteen and a half. My periods started five years ago. They told me I was early. I was ten then, so I'm fifteen now …'

She counts so as not to fall asleep. The jewellery lent her by the negafates *is heavy, the embroidered caftan is heavy, her make-up is heavy, the air she breathes is heavy. The sound of the festivities is soothing. She is ready. Ready to take the hand of her husband, this stranger, this scion of a prominent family, this man whose face and stature are unknown to her. A husband made for her, chosen by her parents, in a sort of pact between people of the same kind. She waits, wrapped in her ceremonial bridal dress, her* seroual *tied too tight. She waits, with no idea what to expect. She tries hard to picture this man naked – pure invention, she's afraid to think beyond that. She's scared, she's thirsty, she isn't hungry, she needs to talk to a married friend and ask her what might happen.*

At around three o'clock in the morning, the head negafa *arrives, a woman whose bulk, natural authority and expression are intimidating, causing girls to look away immediately: 'My girl, you know what's in store for you. It is my duty to initiate you and give you some clear, practical advice. When your husband enters this* dakhchoucha, *you should rise and walk towards him, looking down – never look up at him – and kiss his right hand. Don't hold on to it, let it go, return to the bed and sit down. While he takes off his djellaba, his jabador and his* seroual, *you must wait until he gives you the order to get undressed. In a dark corner of the room, take off your jewellery and then your caftan. Keep on your white* tchamir *and your* seroual, *too – it's up to your husband to remove them. Be careful: no crying out, no tears, this is a crucial moment. A man is going to touch your skin for the first time. Let him have his way, be obedient, gentle and relaxed. Don't be afraid. He will try to penetrate you – open your legs wide, let your mind go blank. It's painful at first. Take this cream and hide it under the pillow. If he has trouble entering you, smear it on your lower lips discreetly, to help things along. When he's inside you, keep him there by wedging your feet under his buttocks. Let him do all the moving. Don't think of enjoying it this night – forget that, my girl – we need to see blood on your white* seroual. *If it hurts, don't cry out. Stifle your cries, yield, endure and, most importantly, prove to each and every one of us that you are a virgin, a daughter from a great family, a girl carrying her family's honour and bringing a flush of pride to their cheeks. That's it, my girl. The first time is painful, but afterwards, when the wound eases and the scar heals, you will never let him go.*

The bridegroom's family announce their arrival with a fanfare, shouts and ululations. Everybody sings: 'He came, he carried her off, he did not forsake her. No, he did not forsake her. He has triumphed! He has triumphed and made her his!' Meanwhile, the negafates *present the bride, bedecked in sparkling jewellery, and demand money before the family will hand her over. The* negafates *chorus: 'See the hostage, see the hostage. Come and deliver her. See the beautiful hostage,* she begs you to deliver her! She is charm, she is beauty, she is reason. See the dates arrayed in mystery, see the pure honey. She is grace, she is soft as the feathers of a dove, she is supple as a reed, she is charm and beauty ...'

The mother steps forward first and tucks a large banknote into the head negafa's belt, followed by the father, who does the same, then the rest of the family, until the negafates consider the ransom sufficient.

It is time to depart. My mother wails, her mother wails, the servants all wail. The noise grows unbearable. It has to be stopped. The night weighs heavy on the heart of this young girl carried off by a man, a stranger, who's about to possess her, make her his wife, make her happy perhaps.

The procession sets off from the house. My mother keeps her eyes down. She thinks she might faint amid the noise and tumult. Her husband takes her hand. Just two streets to cross. She walks, leaning against him. It's the first time a man's hand has held hers. She doesn't think, she lets her mind go blank, she keeps walking, fear in the pit of her stomach, the afternoon's Andalusian music, El Bhiri's band, still ringing in her ears. She sees the hajamas – barbers acting as waiters for the night; she hears all kinds of noise. She walks on, not knowing exactly what awaits her. She feels sick, she gulps, her hands are clammy. She's afraid she'll panic and run away, like her first cousin, who fled when the man took off his seroual and his penis advanced towards her like a stick. The family all laugh when they tell the story. The girl's mother gave chase,

40

slapped her and took her back to the dakhchoucha, *under the guard of the* negafates.

No, she won't flee, she'll let it happen, wait until it's over and, as soon as there's blood on the sheet, she'll go and hide behind the curtains. She dreams of her dolls, made from rags and matchboxes. She dreams of the holidays in Ifrane, at her uncle's house. She thinks of Ali, the cousin who teases her, the one she played brides and grooms with when she was seven. She thinks about her parents, what people will say. She closes her eyes and reluctantly opens her legs, clenching her teeth. Not a word, not a cry. She faints. She is elsewhere, no longer there in that dakhchoucha, *scented with rose water and musk, guarded by a squadron of* negafates. *She's somewhere else, in the cornfields, jumping from terrace to terrace, flying over Fez, disappearing into the blue of the sky. Something like a biting, pinching sensation, then she feels warm liquid trickle between her thighs.*

The next day is the sbohi. *All went well, so they say. The husband sent trays to his new bride's family piled high with dried fruit and nuts: a sign of satisfaction.*

My mother never told me about her wedding. She kept it a secret: there are things you don't tell your children. My grandmother told me a little about it, when I was very young. After the sbohi, *after the second night, my mother, like all young brides, was put through her paces by her mother-in-law, who had arranged for the delivery of three large shad – the migratory fish that swim up the Sebou in spring, the fish with a thousand and one bones and a very particular taste,*

41

which are notoriously difficult to cook. My mother rolled up her sleeves, assuming her place in the kitchen, where no one was allowed to help. She spent all morning cleaning the three fish and then marinated them in a sauce made from coriander, cumin, mild paprika and spicy paprika, a little garlic, salt and pepper. She cooked some of the fish in a tagine and fried the rest in a light oil. At around one o'clock in the afternoon, the two dishes were placed in a tbak and conveyed to her in-laws, accompanied by a large tray of plump Medjool dates and a basket of seasonal fruit.

My mother did not eat that day. She had no appetite. She waited for the plates to be returned. Towards the end of the afternoon, a negafa came to the house singing the call to the Prophet, following it with ululations. The plates had come back, with gifts. At last! My mother had passed the test. Her mother-in-law had no reason to worry: her son would be well fed! After the seventh day, relaxed and happy now, the families met again. The husband took his wife to live in a little house next to his parental home.

10

My mother has always cared about the way she looks. She's never worn dark colours, she loves white, pale yellow, beige. She believes colours should make the heart beat faster, that you shouldn't darken things: a soothing colour is an opening up to life. She used to take especial care in choosing her headscarves, of which she had many. I don't recall ever seeing my mother with her hair flying in the wind or without a scarf. One time, when she was asleep in the hospital, her headscarf slipped, revealing some white hair. I looked away; she wouldn't have wanted me to see it.

My mother doesn't like being in dimly lit rooms. She demands light. She says: 'Light opens and calms the heart. It's a sign of joy, a sign of generosity.' One of my uncles was very frugal, miserly even, a few candles were enough to light his house. He lived in the dark. His wife, too, was afraid of light, of any brightness. They were people who didn't like to show themselves in daylight. Terrified of the evil eye, they lived a semi-clandestine existence in the belief that other people looking at them could only bring harm. So, no light. My mother didn't like going to their house, though she accepted this foible and all their petty-mindedness. When they came to our house, they were amazed to see so much light. My uncle would say: 'What a waste! All these light bulbs really aren't necessary. We don't need that much light just to see each other.' My mother didn't like mean people, but she'd never criticise. She'd say: 'Everyone lives as they choose. I don't judge. I'd rather not spend time with people who think money's more important than human beings. Money's what our ancestors thought of as the dirt of life, the debris of time. So I hope people who hoard it know that there's no room for bank accounts in a coffin!' She'd laugh about it, although she was sorry not to have enough money herself to live better.

Mother's naive and takes herself seriously. She loves to laugh but she interprets everything literally. Father would tease her. He could be brilliantly funny and sardonic. Some people in the family liked this quick-wittedness, others feared his sharp tongue and kept their distance. My mother didn't like my father's joking. Now, she talks about those days with regret: 'Your father wasn't fair to me. He hurt me but he wasn't a bad man, he worked all his life. He never did well in business, like his friends; it made him bitter and jealous of other people's wealth. I didn't like that in him. He could wound people, not realising how much his sarcasm upset them. Afterwards, he'd be surprised that they were annoyed or cold towards him. He'd speak his mind, didn't keep anything to himself. He was always embarrassing me. Some of our friends would come and see me when they knew he was away travelling. They'd rather not have to see him. The things he'd say! He was so clever, but what's the use of cleverness when it's so brutal and unfeeling?'

My older brother comes to see her twice a week, in the late afternoon. He's very affectionate. As she says, 'He covers me in kisses.' Since he's also unwell, he's careful about his health. He discusses his aches and pains with her, his difficulties with his children. She listens and doesn't judge him. He's a delicate, cultured man, a good Muslim, moderate, with a horror of fanaticism and fundamentalism of any kind. A very sensitive man, he's retreated from life. My mother would rather he hadn't, but she doesn't say anything. She'd have loved to see him happy, generous, open and less anxious. But she finds his presence comforting. Even though she gets him muddled up with me or my other brother. Then she corrects herself and apologises. She knows it hurts us. But no one holds it against her. We all know that her illness plays tricks on her. When she's lucid, she sets the record straight: 'Don't go thinking I've gone mad! It's all the pills I've been taking for over thirty years that have damaged my mind. Add it up: about ten pills a day for thirty years, how many is that? A tonne? Two tonnes? Enough to kill an army! So if I get things wrong, if I don't recognise you straight away, don't be angry with me. It's that wretched medicine that's to blame. The pills have saved me, but at the same time, they've destroyed something inside me.'

When she was in the hospital, with death prowling her room, a cousin suggested taking her back home: 'It would be better for her to pass away in her own house.' The comment reminded me of one of her wishes: 'If I die away from home, please don't make me spend the night in the fridge.' My father had died in the afternoon and spent the night in the morgue. It wasn't until eight o'clock the next morning that the ambulance brought his body back to the house. That cold night had broken my mother's heart. She'd talk about it often. I once tried to tell her that death is the absence of all feeling, but she was adamant that her body, even if devoid of sensation, must not spend the night in the fridge. When we told her that Father had died, she had this strange reaction: 'But where is he?' My brother said: 'At the hospital, in the morgue.' 'You mean in the fridge?' 'Yes, in the fridge, that's the way it's done.' She didn't sleep at all that night. She dressed in white, picked up her beads and began to pray. All night long, she must have been thinking about her husband. I'd even venture that she'd never thought about him as she did that night. She must have identified with him, felt the cold he was unable to feel. She put herself in his place, in that glacial chamber, shivering constantly and feeling sick. Death isn't only the absence of feeling, it's also the thought of nothingness, of what's no longer there,

46

of what's inevitably approaching. Since that night, she's had a horror of being put in the fridge.

11

She was barely sixteen when she fell pregnant. Sidi Mohammed learned it from his mother, who summoned him to break the good news: 'Lalla Fatma is expecting a baby. May God grant it's a boy, but I'll be just as happy with a girl, even though your older brother only has daughters. I can't wait to see your son. Lalla Fatma shows excellent promise – may God protect her and ease the ordeal of pregnancy – she has nothing but good qualities, and she makes delicious tagines. Are you happy, my son?' 'Yes, Mother, I'm very happy. She really is a girl from a good family. Parents such as hers are exceptional.'

In her seventh month of pregnancy, Sidi Mohammed fell ill. His complexion looked sallow, he lost weight, and often had a raging fever. He no longer went out. The nurse, Drissi, came to his bedside, and was unable to hide his despondency: 'He is in God's hands. It's a scourge afflicting our country. I hope

I'm wrong. I've given him a nice, strong injection to make him sleep. Don't wake him. I'll see you tomorrow. God is merciful!'

My mother cried. The entire family was with him. When Sidi Mohammed awoke, he looked dazed, his eyes were glassy and he had difficulty speaking. The worst of it was that, several times a day, lamentations for the dead rang out as funeral processions passed by. The typhus epidemic had spread. Drissi worked without pause. Another nurse, Skalli, went from house to house handing out white pills. The corpse washers were busy day and night.

Drissi advised that Lalla Fatma should be kept away from Sidi Mohammed until the birth. My mother refused to leave her husband, or her home. Lalla Radhia, the midwife, insisted she follow her. Touria was born just as her father breathed his last: he never set eyes on her. My mother cried throughout. Someone even dared say that she'd brought bad luck. My mother didn't leave her parents' house. It was her mother who looked after Touria for those first months, she nursed her alongside my mother's baby sister.

Sidi Mohammed was buried in El Guebeb cemetery. He was just twenty-one years old. My mother visited his grave every Friday and spoke to him: 'Touria looks just like you, she has your eyes, your skin, and your gentleness. It was God's will, there's nothing we can do! I pray every day that you're on the way to paradise, that you forgive me if, in a moment of distraction, I failed in my duty. Now I pray to God each day that your child will grow up in good health and in joy. I'll make

*an offering to Moulay Idriss, so our Prophet's companions will
welcome you as you deserve! Thanks be to God!'*

'I'm not afraid of death,' she likes to repeat. 'Death is a right
that God bestows. I'm not talking about divine will. And
illness is another thing. It's death that's the coward. It stalks
us, goes for one part of our body, tortures it, takes away its
natural function, then travels round, takes on another part,
savages it, makes it suffer, and in the end attacks the mind.
I'm not afraid of death, but of seeing my suffering reflected
in your eyes; it's seeing you overcome with grief because
I'm suffering, eaten up from the inside. That I can't bear. I
believe, I surrender to God and I'm glad He's calling me to
Him. But I have one wish: for you all to be there, and for you
not to suffer.'

My mother's never heard of homes where old people are
parked. She couldn't imagine for a second that one of her
children might throw her out, exile her somewhere. Whether
it's called 'home', 'hospice', 'rest home' or 'retirement home',
it's a dumping ground. I was very moved by a Japanese film
I saw, in which an old man is carried to the top of a snow-
covered mountain to hasten his death. I think it's a tradition
that derives from excessive pride on the part of the elderly,
who are loath to be a burden to their offspring. They cry
out for this exile among birds of prey. They're left on the
mountainside and everyone goes home, slightly relieved
and slightly sad. In a country where suicide is common,
where people have a strong sense of honour, the elderly pre-

empt what's coming, and their children's meanness: they go before they're unwanted. The idea's quite appealing in theory, but when it comes to the act, it's monstrous – a form of euthanasia, but more perverse. As soon as a person's no longer productive or becomes mentally incapacitated, they must make way for the younger generation.

In Morocco, besides the love of God, we're taught an almost religious reverence for our parents. The worst thing that can happen to someone is that their parents disown them. To refuse to give a child your blessing is to exile them to a place without mercy – to abandon them, discard them like a worthless object. It's to withdraw all trust and, worst of all, to close the door of your house to them, the door to life and hope. It's the most severe humiliation and isolation. We live in fear of one day being denied our parents' blessing. This blessing is a reassuring symbol, a soothing tradition. We owe our parents this submission, which in the west might seem ridiculous, or psychologically unacceptable. I've always kissed my father's and my mother's right hand. I've never dared smoke in front of them, never shouted or sworn. It's the way we're brought up, the way we are with those we love. That doesn't mean there are no problems or arguments, but we cultivate love above all. On our parents' side, that love can be all-consuming and possessive, it can be irritating and stifling. But that does not justify a fundamental lack of respect, a respect that involves affection, an almost irrational surrender. That's what filial love is, a bond that can't be quantified. You accept it as life's gift and do your utmost to be worthy and proud of it.

When you love your parents, you don't get rid of them. I remember a scene from an Italian comedy in which Alberto Sordi takes his elderly mother out in his new car, its seats still covered in plastic. He buys her an ice-cream and promises her a lovely drive. Unused to such solicitude from her self-centred, rather awful son, she's obviously worried. She realises he's taking her to an old people's home. Which he does – cynically, cruelly, and smiling throughout. This contemptible son leaves with the tiniest twinge of conscience, a sadness that lasts no more than a moment. We, the audience, were choked. I identified with the poor old woman: my eyes filled with tears. Then I tried to put myself in the son's shoes, and I felt sick. Yet this scene has become routine, is the norm in the west. People are no longer indignant: it's just the way things are. They blame lack of space, lack of time. They take refuge in easy selfishness, which these same parents will pass on to their children: the wheel keeps turning in the eternal cycle of a modernity that will sacrifice old people even as it seeks to prolong their life expectancy. This paradox is the inevitable result of a society in which the only values celebrated and protected are those of the market.

Morocco, which has been influenced by the European lifestyle, will resist. Perhaps it won't build old people's homes. One day, probably in the distant future, a young, dynamic property developer will build a complex of small houses for the elderly. He'll present it with panache: 'Our parents deserve to be taken care of – not just any old how, we're not having them sleep in with the children – they deserve comfort and calm. They'll be happy in these apartments, designed specially for those who wish to grow old in peace. Which doesn't mean they'll be forgotten, oh no, not at all. I am myself a child whose success has only been possible because of his parents' blessing. No, we're going to look after them: a trained nurse will visit, an experienced doctor too – they'll have everything to hand. In their twilight years, our parents will enjoy peace of mind and conditions of material comfort that are second to none ...'

And he'll find a few unscrupulous offspring to buy into his vision. Fashion and selfishness will do the rest.

12

One morning, I took advantage of a lucid interval to ask my mother what she thought of the practice.

'You mean I wouldn't live in my own house any more?'

'You'd be in a house where specially trained people would look after you. You'd lack for nothing – you'd have doctors close at hand, and your nurse, and your children would come and see you from time to time.'

'From time to time? That means the time would be counted. But what about Keltum, who's been with me for fifteen years, she'd be there, wouldn't she?'

'No, she's not ill and she's not old.'

'And why would I want to leave here? You're planning to sell the house? That's what it is. You can't wait to inherit.'

'No, I was joking. I just wanted you to know that in other countries, like France or Spain, they put old people in special homes. I knew you'd react like that.'

'My house is good enough for me, I don't need a special home. I won't ever leave it. I'll go to my grave from this room, and then you can do what you like. You can even demolish the house, or turn it into a block of flats. But I like it here and I'm staying.'

Mother wasn't joking. Even when she was well, she'd only reluctantly agree to go and spend a few days with her daughter in Fez or her son in Casablanca. She's deeply attached to the house, the symbol of essential and indisputable rootedness. Whatever my father's financial difficulties, he'd always insisted on owning his house. You can go hungry, but you mustn't be on the streets, without a roof over your head. In Fez, growing up, everyone had to own their own house. The people who rented were from the country, they weren't city-dwellers. I remember we used to rent out part of our house in Makhfiya to people from Fasjdid, on the outskirts of Fez. A sheet was hung in the hallway to separate the two families. We were on the ground floor and they had the upstairs and the terrace. It was a big house, but we all took care not to cause problems. We couldn't make ends meet without the rental income. Renting rooms was frowned upon in bourgeois families, but my father wasn't ashamed to admit that we were humble people, poor even.

Yesterday, for the first time, my mother didn't recognise my voice on the phone, and worse, she started ranting. She took me for her younger brother, Moulay Ali, who'd died twenty years before. She was furious:

'Aren't you ashamed, Moulay Ali? Your sister's ill and you've never come to see her? Where are you? You're hiding! Your wife's still giving the orders and she won't let you come and see me. That's not right.'

'But Yemma, this is your son, Tahar!'

'No, Tahar's gone to give his daughter's hand in marriage. He's not in Morocco. And you, who are you? Ah, you're Mustafa, the son who went away, who abandoned me ...'

'No, Yemma, Moulay Ali died a long time ago.'

'Oh, I see! He died and no one told me. That's not very nice.'

She didn't remain a widow for long. Her uncle, Sidi Abdesslam, spoke with her father. 'She's so young, so innocent and beautiful, and her hands are exquisite. She mustn't stay cloistered in your house, she should go out, accompany her mother to the weddings she's invited to – that's where she'll be noticed. The other day I had a visit from Sidi Abdelkrim, a wealthy man who's married but his wife is ill. He has four grown-up children with her, but he's still in his prime. He asked me to approach you. He would be delighted if you offered him Lalla Fatma's hand. I know you'll tell me he's old enough to be her father, that she'll have to live with the sick woman, maybe even look after her, but let me tell you it will be quite the opposite: she's young and beautiful, she'll be the favourite, she'll be the only one. The other wife, poor thing, is so ill she isn't even aware of her surroundings. The boys are grown-up, they're all traders and they look after Sidi Abdelkrim's assets. What do you think? What answer should I give?'

And that was how she remarried. It was a discreet ceremony, there were no festivities. The two families gathered in Sidi Abdesslam's big house. The aduls *drew up the new marriage certificate on the same sheet of paper. After the death of Sidi Mohammed – may God bless him and show him mercy – after the end of the waiting and mourning period, after discussions between the families, Moulay Ahmed consented to give the widow Lalla Fatma in matrimony to Sidi Abdelkrim, who was already married and the father of four children. The 5,000-rial* sadaqah *was handed over to the father of the bride. They all agreed there should be no celebrations. The widow Lalla Fatma would move into her new husband's house once the marriage was registered. May God Almighty protect them and give them His blessing.*
Fatha.
Amen.

She moved to a different neighbourhood and it took her a while to adjust to her new life. She thought about her first husband all the time and prayed to God that her life would no longer be dogged by misfortune.

Sidi Abdelkrim treated her like a princess. He made a fuss of her, gave her servants, and asked her not to wear herself out or to go into the kitchen, which was the preserve of Ghita, the black cook brought back from Senegal by Sidi Abdelkrim's father some time around 1915.

Pregnant again, she allowed herself to be pampered and did not exert herself. Life went quietly by. The other wife liked her and advised her on ways to please and always satisfy Sidi Abdelkrim: 'My illness has me bedridden. These days I can hardly move. Luckily, Ghita takes good care of me: I couldn't let the house go uncared for, every morning she comes to my room and I give her instructions. I am fond of you, you know. You're from a very good family. Thank you for being here, for consenting to marry an older man, especially one who's already married. It was I who asked him to find another wife, as our religion demands: that is Sharia law. I said to him, "My dear Sidi Abdelkrim, you can't go on without a woman in your bed. God allows you up to four wives, you absolutely must remarry. If I enjoyed good health, I wouldn't ask it of you, but like this I'm no use to you, I'm just a worthless old thing. My children have grown up – may God bless them and keep them – they won't oppose a second marriage. Take a wife – a widow or a divorcee. Typhus has killed so many young men, there must be a pretty young widow to share my beloved husband's bed!"

'You know, he kissed both my hands then went off to speak with your uncle. You are welcome here, may you bring us the goodness and health we have lacked for some time. Lalla Fatma, can you help me sit up? Take my hand, pull, gently, that's right, put this pillow behind me. My back has to be supported or I'll be in pain. All my muscles hurt, it's difficult to move my hand, especially my fingers. Usually it's Ghita who cares for me, who bathes and dresses me, and feeds me like a baby … I'm happy to have some company. So give us a fine boy. And be quick about it, the house needs new life and the laughter of children. My adult sons are married, they come and see me every day. But their wives drag their feet, they don't like it here, which means I don't see my granddaughters very often.

'No one knows what this illness is called. Drissi, the nurse, tells me it's a kind of rheumatism, because of the cold and damp in Fez. I worked like a slave for years, I ruined my health in that enormous kitchen. My husband, our husband – may God keep him – loves to entertain. He was always inviting friends to lunch and would only ever tell me the same morning. Can you imagine how hard that was? Everything had to be done in a hurry, rushing around, not forgetting to make the bread. Ghita helped, but my husband insisted I do the cooking myself. He'd say: "Your hands work miracles, don't deprive us of their creations."

'So tell me, what did your husband die of?'
'Of the disease with a name I don't want to utter in this happy household. He was carried off in a matter of weeks. I watched him waste away day after day. Only his big, very dark eyes stayed the same. I was pregnant, I had morning sickness, I didn't feel well, and I said to myself that my arrival in this family hadn't kept misfortune at bay. I couldn't sleep, spent

all my time crying. When my daughter was born, my mother took her from me. I was too weak and too unhappy to care for her. I left her with my mother. My little sister's only eighteen months older than her. It was my mother who nursed her. It's as if I hadn't had a child.'

Sidi Abdelkrim was very attentive to his new wife. He forbade her from setting foot in the kitchen, saying: 'I don't want these pretty little hands to be ruined by work. You are my princess, my gazelle, a gift from God, I want you to be happy. I can feel your body's changing. Is it carrying another gift from God? I hope so.'

She gave birth to a boy: seven days of celebrations. Sidi Abdelkrim's sick wife wept with joy. The child was named Abdel Aziz. The father wanted to call him Abdel Razzaq, as a reminder that this gift from God was precious.

My mother thinks she had twins: she talks of Hassan and Houcine. Her son Abdel Aziz laughs at her and tells her she's thinking of her cousin, who did in fact give birth to twins the same week.

Now she's asking for her husband, who died over fifty years ago. She says she needs to speak to him. We remind her that he's no longer with us. 'Oh, I see! You're hiding things from me!'

Abdel Aziz was brought up in that huge house by a mother who was too young and a stepmother who was ill. As soon as he was old enough to go to school, his older brother took him to live in his house. His father, who was elderly and ailing, no longer went out. Now Drissi the nurse almost never left the house. They brought in Hammad, their blind cousin, who was famous for his beautiful recitation of the Qur'an. In the family, they knew the arrival of Hammad meant that death was approaching. Sidi Abdelkrim passed away in his sleep. Two months later, screaming in pain, his first wife died. A widow again, my mother appealed to Moulay Idriss, whose mausoleum she visited every Thursday. She'd bring offerings, and would stay there for hours, praying and entreating God to show her His great mercy and compassion. She returned to live in her parents' house and was reunited with her daughter, by now aged eight. Marrying again was out of the question – she was convinced she was a harbinger of doom, of death, a victim of fate and the evil eye. She'd gaze up at the sky, tracking and talking to the stars.

13

This morning she's beaming, asking for a mirror and lipstick. 'Quick, quick, Keltum, all three of them are coming for lunch. They met at the Moulay Idriss mausoleum at Friday prayers, and decided to come and eat a *mrouzia* tagine, one of my specialities. Quick, Keltum, bring me the pot. Have you marinated the meat? Don't forget the seven spices, it's getting late ...'

Out of curiosity, Keltum asks her who are these people coming to lunch. 'My three husbands, of course. Yes, my three men, they're here in Fez. They're coming after midday prayers and the house isn't ready. I'm starting to worry. Nothing's ready, I'm so ashamed. What am I going to do? What will I tell them?'

Luckily, a moment later she forgets, and takes up the usual thread of her life. She asks for her medication, complains about Keltum's laziness, adjusts her clothes and begins to pine for the days when she was stylish and beautiful. Then, driven by the devil, she's off again:

'Last night, before I went to bed, I opened my suitcase and counted my dresses and caftans. There were seven of them. I put them there, by my pillow. I wanted to sleep knowing my things were there, within reach. In the morning, they'd gone. Yes, gone. I'm surrounded by wicked people, by thieves. My dresses and caftans are nowhere to be found. Keltum must have sold them at auction. It's like the pills – especially the expensive ones – she steals them and sells them. I don't have proof, but I know how greedy country people can be; they're never satisfied. They're jealous. You see, son, the moment you go, they do exactly as they please; they leave me here, all alone. I cry out, I shout, but they don't come. I can't say a word to them; at the least little thing, they just drop everything and leave. It frightens me. You, you understand me. Do something, so they won't abandon me. Now, where did my shoes go?'

'But Yemma, you've got a bad foot, it's covered in a dressing and won't fit in your shoe.'

'No, I want to be sure my shoes haven't been sold.'

'No one's sold anything.'

'Oh good. I'm so tired. Can you give me some money, to buy … What do I need to buy? I've forgotten. Oh lord, my memory's gone, I'm forgetting everything. Your father used to tease me, saying I couldn't even remember what we'd had for supper the night before. He was exaggerating, but sometimes I did have trouble remembering things.'

Keltum's curiosity got the better of her again. That afternoon, while we were having tea, she asked: 'Is it true you had three husbands?'

'I don't know. My foot hurts. I need a painkiller and you're talking to me about marriage. No, I've decided I won't marry again.'

She won't marry again, she'll never get married again ...

The Diwane is the heart of the medina in Fez. That's where all the shops are huddled together. That's where Moulay Abdesslam, my mother's uncle, would meet my father and become his closest friend. My father imported spices wholesale: crates and jute sacks were brought to the Diwane on the backs of mules. Sacks of coriander seeds, cumin from Africa, saffron from Spain, ginger from Asia, paprika, chilli pepper, white pepper, black pepper, tea from China, green tea, black tea ... Moulay Abdesslam, who sold babouches, liked to come and smell the spices: he helped my father put away the stock, chatting all the while. That was how he learned that my father was neither happy nor satisfied with his wife, who was unable to bear him children.

'You need a wife, a proper wife, one who's already had children!'

'Not so easy to come by, Moulay Abdesslam. My mother, who could have looked for a new wife for me, is no longer with us, alas, so I suffer in silence.'

'We must remedy that, my dear friend!'

'How?'

'Leave it to me. I won't say anything now. I'll ask around, and let you know.'

That was how Moulay Abdesslam persuaded his brother, who had to persuade his wife, who had to speak to my mother and ask if she'd agree to be the second wife of a fine man, a spice merchant from a good family.

I don't know which of the four had the idea of laying down a proviso for the marriage: the wedding would go ahead on condition that he divorce his first wife as soon as Lalla Fatma fell pregnant.

The agreement was concluded and a token dowry arranged. There was a small celebration, and my mother came to live with the first wife, who was convinced her husband was impotent. He'd spend one night with one wife, one night with the other, until the day ululations echoed through the house: my mother was pregnant. She had her first morning sickness, her first cravings; she was crowned queen and the other wife left of her own accord. My father sent her his 'letter', in other words his repudiation.

The house seemed bigger, immense. My father, who was very solicitous, never came home empty-handed.

The traders in the Diwane learned the news. Si Hassan is expecting a child, and his first wife is seeking another husband.

Maalem Zitouni, the butcher of the Rcif neighbourhood, was tired of being single. A young divorcee wouldn't turn up her nose at him. No easy matter, a woman agreeing to share the bed of a butcher, who, whatever he did, would always smell of fat and blood. Moulay Abdesslam agreed to act as go-between. There was a big wedding, a big celebration, and a good dowry was arranged.

Meanwhile, my mother gave birth to a boy.

Fez suffered in the Great War: oil, sugar and flour were rationed and there was little demand for spices. Daily life was hard, but my father was the happiest of men. His young wife was expecting a second child. He would say: 'This child will bring peace, there'll be no more war, I'm sure of it!'

I came into the world a few months before the end of the war.

The butcher's wife gave birth to twins.

14

I've often wondered whether she and my father loved each other. They shared an affection, yes, but passionate love, with romantic declarations, gifts, flowers and tender words, no. They got on each other's nerves. My father was always saying that his wife didn't understand him, she upset him, annoyed him, showed him no respect. My mother, who was less vindictive, criticised his lack of generosity, his aggressiveness, and said he was unfeeling. They'd often argue … very often. My mother would cry, call on us as witnesses, and demand our support, even our protection. My father would protest, saying that he was 'alone in his camp', and we were on our mother's side. There was no cruelty or physical violence, it was more a question of incompatible temperaments. There was too great a gulf between them. He called her ignorant and illiterate. She could neither read nor write. She'd learned two phone numbers, one of which was for my father's shop. She'd dial it from memory. He'd laugh at her, he could be very sarcastic. He'd trip her up and find her confusion amusing. Then she'd sulk. He couldn't understand why she wasn't talking to him, he'd try anything to restore the peace. Silence was my mother's weapon. Whenever he fell ill, with flu or a stomach bug, she'd call us in a panic. She'd worry at the slightest thing. When he died, she observed the traditional mourning rituals. I suspected part of her was relieved. Naturally, she wouldn't talk about it or let anything show. From time to time she'd mention him, saying he'd been a good man, a decent man, who'd been unlucky in his working life.

My parents were simple people who quietly accepted the ancestral tradition according to which you did not show feelings or emotions in public. They were both reserved, not in the habit of expressing their affection in words.

Because he hated social and religious hypocrisy, my father tended towards the anarchic and liked to provoke. Mother was more diplomatic. She was forever making amends for the damage caused by things my father had said. People loved her for it and respected her sense of proportion. She never spoke badly of others. Even when she was cheated by the women who worked for her, or fell out with cousins or neighbours, she'd put herself in God's hands and ask Him to mete out justice. Such fatalism, such serenity and goodness shielded her from malicious gossip. No one badmouthed her. She was said to have inherited her kindness from her father. The same could not be said of my father, who was never afraid to speak his mind. He made no concessions to anyone, living or dead, whether they were close to him or not. It occupied and amused him to let nothing go unremarked. He kept a big notebook and he'd write down everything: births, baptisms, circumcisions, weddings, deaths and especially what things cost. Flicking through it, you learned the history of the family and the mood of the times. This notebook, filled with detailed, sometimes acerbic comments, made various uncles and cousins tremble. The women couldn't keep their dates of birth secret, or exaggerate the amount paid for their jewellery. He knew everything and had no compunction about writing it all down. That was how I discovered that my father had tried everything he could to have children with his first wife. In those days, there was no doctor in the medina, only a nurse who treated everyone. People had confidence in him and, when things looked serious, they entrusted themselves to God. The nurse, Drissi, told him that God was against this union, that their marriage was a mistake. He should repudiate this wife and give her her freedom. That was when he began to discuss matters with Sidi Abdesslam.

It was all written down in the big notebook: the discussion with my mother's uncle, the hesitations, the crucial precondition ...

'I saw Sidi Abdesslam this morning. He's a good man, fat and very helpful. I confided in him. My wife is barren. We've been married over two years

69

and her belly is still empty. Without children, life is meaningless. I'm from a family of seven – five boys and two girls. Sidi Abdesslam spoke very highly of Lalla Fatma, his niece. I don't know what she's like, if she's difficult and capricious, or meek and obedient. I won't stand for a rebellious wife. That's just how I am. I've already told him that, but he reassured me. Lalla Fatma is from a very good family, well brought-up, her father is respected and loved. They aren't rich. But what does that matter! I hope the business will be concluded very quickly.'

How many times did I try to find out how it all happened? Impossible! Her memory loss, perhaps, or a refusal to disclose certain facts. These days, Mother has little interest in that time. She prefers to talk about her first husband, the one who died a few months after their wedding. As for the second, the one she calls 'the old man', she recounts her escapades, and running away: 'I was just a girl. My mother was bringing up my daughter Touria along with my little sister, Amina. I didn't worry about what was going on at home. As soon as I had the chance, I'd escape and go back to my parents. My father would grab me by the hand and take me back to the old man. He didn't dare be angry with me, given the vast age difference. I had a son with that man. A few months later, he died of old age; I was a widow again, and I was relieved. I didn't dislike him, but I didn't understand what I was doing there. I was alone for a few years, maybe a year, I can't remember, and then Uncle Sidi Abdesslam came to suggest I remarry. I knew my father was behind my uncle's approach. I couldn't say no; you didn't do that in those days. I married your father without ever having seen him. It was the same with the two previous husbands. People married without having met, without even laying eyes on one another. It was like a lottery, a complete surprise. In the beginning, your father was sweet as honey, very gentle, especially when I became pregnant. He sent the other wife away and there I was with a very loving, very attentive man. So that was it, it all happened just as I say, everything went smoothly, there was no problem. Later, our relationship had its difficulties. You knew that. You saw them. Anyway, let's forget all that now.'

My mother sent for a plumber and an electrician. She asked them to overhaul the entire system. The wash-basin tap was changed and light bulbs replaced. Now, everything is in order: the house is clean, the walls repainted. A dust-covered chandelier in a sorry state hangs in the middle of the sitting room. My mother hasn't noticed it. All the bulbs went long ago. We no longer even see it. It's a relic from the days when my father bought things at the flea market. The chandelier's worthless. We could get rid of it, throw it out or give it to the rubbish collectors. But then we'd have to find a ladder, take it down, and undo the wires holding it in place. It's better to forget about it.

The plumber and the electrician were part of the plan to get the house ready to receive the entire family on the day of her funeral. My mother's obsessed with this ceremony. I'm no longer surprised when she tells me the reception must be a splendid affair: 'It'll be the last time my family comes over, so it might as well be elegant and grand. No penny-pinching or cutting corners: buy free-range chickens, not the ones stuffed with drugs to make them fatter. Buy white tablecloths. Don't forget about sheets for the people who'll stay the night. If it's winter, get out the blankets. I want everyone to be happy. Do it as if I were still here, alive, smiling at you and laughing. I love entertaining, and doing it well. I know you'll make a real occasion of it – I don't have any worries about that. But I'll say it and say it again: don't you make me blush in my grave!'

Mother hasn't cooked for some time. Even when ill, she'd position herself next to Keltum and dictate what to cook. These days, she's given up any involvement with food. But in her mind, she's the one who cooks, through Keltum. It's hard to tell her the tagine's no good or the minced meat is too spicy. She takes it badly, convinced that Keltum is the extension of her culinary skills. I don't like Keltum's cooking. It's too oily, and has no subtlety. I refuse to believe I'm eating my mother's food. I pretend. I ask for simple things: grilled meat and salads. For my mother, to eat her food is to love her. If I sometimes didn't finish what was on my plate, she'd sigh and fret. To eat is to celebrate a strong, indissoluble emotional bond.

Over the past few months, Mother's lost interest in eating. She merely picks at the food on her plate. She says she eats so she can swallow her many pills. Only Keltum knows her drug regime. Although she's illiterate, she has her own little tricks to help her tell the packets of tablets apart and give my mother her medication at the right time. She says: 'The little pink pill is for your heart, to be taken every morning. The two white ones are for your blood pressure, to be taken before lunch. At night, there's the green box, then the blue one, and half a red pill to help you sleep.' Mother trusts her completely. She's just afraid that Keltum will fall ill and make a mistake in the dosage, or simply forget altogether.

Mother claims she no longer dreams. She forgets, that's all. On the other hand, she cherishes her hallucinations. For over a month, she hasn't stopped telling us the story of the sparrow that came to her window one night and began to call out the different names for Allah. She interpreted this visit as a sign from heaven telling her she should prepare to depart this life. Mother repeated the names after the sparrow and the prayers it sang. She said it came, tapped on the window and spoke to her directly. My sister Touria confirmed the vision and there was nothing more to say.

Ever since Touria lost her husband in a car accident, she can suddenly faint, fall to the floor and lie unconscious, with her eyes open. Completely gone. The doctor mentioned hysteria. When she comes to, she reassures us: 'It's nothing, it's always happening, just like that, out of the blue. It comes from up above, from God, there's nothing to be done. Even the doctors agree, we just have to wait for the moment to pass. In the beginning, the children were frightened, they thought I was dying, but now they're used to it. I keel over and no one notices me, that's just how it is, no need to panic. I simply need to rest, maybe to go to Mecca again, but how would I manage it? Without him, I couldn't. We always did everything hand in hand, with never a cross word. We never argued. I listened to him and he listened to me. We got along as if we were made of the same stuff. The truth is, I can't live without him, even though I have my children and they look after me. Well, you have to forget, make as if you're carrying on.'

Mother is aware her daughter's behaviour has grown increasingly strange: 'It got worse when her poor husband died. He loved me like his own mother. He was a good man, generous and principled. If a little rigid. When he said no it was no. What a disaster, such a cruel, brutal death! It was written. He died on impact. A lorry pulled out from a line of cars and ploughed straight into him. If he'd agreed to put off leaving until the next day, the lorry would have driven into another car. Dear God, forgive me. It was written, since the day he was born. He was stubborn. If he'd listened to me, he wouldn't be dead. Oh Lord, forgive me, I'm rambling. It's all in Your hands: life, death, joy, tears, everything. We're nothing on this earth. I must pray now. I haven't done my ablutions. Where's the polished stone for washing myself? They're stealing everything, they're robbing me while I'm still alive. Even what's-her-name, she took my gold earrings and the necklace with the pendant. It's unbelievable, people's greed. As if God doesn't give us enough of His goodness. Where was I? Oh, Mother's in Fez and she's refusing to drive to see me. But where are we? What city are we living in? Tangier, you say? But Tangier was another time, I wasn't yet married. I'm getting it all muddled up. My mother won't come! Although I'm her daughter, she'd rather stay with my little sister. She's always preferred Amina. Her husband's rich. I'm the eldest and still she neglects me. It's isn't nice.'

All day she called her daughter 'Yemma'.

On the phone, Mother easily recognises me. The voice must be imprinted deeper in the memory than the face. In fact, she sometimes mistakes me for one of my brothers. The other day, she commented that my voice had broken: 'You have a man's voice. You've grown up fast. You're my little one, my little youngest one. I love all my children but with you there's something more. That's just the way it is, I don't know why. You mustn't be angry with me. When are you coming to see me? Be careful how you walk, don't forget you're only a child!'

My mother's sent me back to childhood. In her eyes, I haven't grown up. I'm still the child she adored in Fez when I was ill and wasting away right before her eyes. She's returned to the time when she was afraid of losing me to a mysterious disease. I tell her I'm over fifty, I have four children and she must be confusing her son with her grandsons. She only half-believes me: 'That's right, tell me I'm crazy, I'm losing my mind, your mother's inventing things. Yes, give me a sign if you agree. Maybe you're right, I'm raving. You know, pills don't just do good, they destroy what they don't heal. So you aren't my little boy and we aren't in Fez. But what's this new house then? I don't know it. Take me back home. You're not going to leave me here, are you?'

My sister has left. She ran out of patience, looking after Mother. She just snapped. I understood, and told her to take care of her health. She replied that all is in God's hands. I said nothing and looked down. What can you say to those who believe in fate, who think everything is written in advance and that we are on earth only to follow the path traced for us by God? Mother's less fatalistic than her daughter. She's convinced that God determines human actions but that we shouldn't sit idly by, just waiting for things to happen.

15

The cardiologist has come this morning. He asks me to help him raise my mother up so he can examine her. She's not very heavy. As I lean over, I catch a glimpse of her left breast. Withered, emptied, flabby skin. I look away and wish I hadn't seen it. I shouldn't have stayed in the room. My mother always had beautiful breasts. One of my sunniest childhood memories comes back to me. We were in Fez. I was playing on the terrace when my mother suddenly appeared: she was looking for me, thinking I'd run off somewhere. She didn't have much on, and I clearly saw her magnificent breasts. I must have been five or six years old. She hugged me to her and kissed my head. My eyes were buried in her chest. I pressed against her; it was soft and soothing.

That memory is far more vivid than the ones from the hammam. Of course, I've seen my mother naked several times, but mostly in the steam and semi-darkness of the

Turkish baths. There were other women, other shapes that assailed me at night: I often had nightmares in which my head was being crushed by two immense breasts, or my puny body trapped between heavy, sticky thighs. No, I don't have good memories of those times in the hammam. I was relieved when *l'Assise,* the woman who always sat at the door, stopped me going in. My mother tried to protest, but I was too old to be innocent. That's what *l'Assise* said. So I waited outside. I loved watching the women coming out, smelling of soap, henna and perfume.

My mother rarely wore make-up. She's never bought a brand-name lipstick. When she was well, she'd use an artisanal product that made her cheeks too pink. She's never heard of foundation or anti-wrinkle creams, let alone cosmetic surgery. Wouldn't know it exists. Someone told her that one of her nieces had had a nose job and a breast job. She laughed and asked God to forgive her. 'How can you touch God's work? It's heresy.' Then she added: 'That's why she has suddenly aged! It's God's punishment!'

My mother knows that her body has succumbed to disease, but she doesn't complain, doesn't hanker after her lost youth. She has no regrets, just a slight weariness at having to come to terms with a weak body and increasingly blurred eyesight. She doesn't hide her age. And has no idea when she was born. 'I'm old, I'm at death's door. That's how it is, it's our fate. I'm not afraid, just tired of waiting. But I need you all there when I go. That's all I ask!'

I've sometimes tried to work out how old she is by cross-referencing people's accounts with historical events. Married the first time at a very young age, her memory of that time is vague. The fact is, she doesn't care about the passing of time. She just says that sometimes she ran away from her husband's house to go and play dolls with her cousins. In the evening, her husband would come and fetch her but didn't have the heart to reprimand her. She must have been fifteen. Of course, he was rather older. They hadn't met before the wedding night. That was how it was in those days, a matter of tradition, of modesty. No one spoke about it. Who would have dared question that sort of custom? In her family, not one woman of her generation rebelled against it.

I remember the afternoons when the women would gather in our big house in Fez. They'd drink tea and bake cakes, they'd be laughing and joking, using swear words, and forget I was there. I'd pretend to be asleep. They referred to men's penises. Some of them got to their feet and danced. My mother was very reserved. Her younger sister was more daring. Using the almond paste for the gazelle-horn biscuits, she once modelled a huge penis and testicles, rolled it in flour and sent it to the ovens. The women fought over who would eat it. I laughed quietly in my corner.

I've always loved sitting beside my mother, listening to her. Before, she'd tell me about her life when she was young, or the difficulties of married life. She didn't resent my father, but was sad that he showed her so little affection. She noticed how well her sister was treated by her husband and it made

79

her slightly envious. But very quickly, as if she'd offended fate, she'd ask God's forgiveness and pray for His help to endure difficult things: 'Lord, I know I had a bad thought. I strayed into ignorance and followed the devil, so please forgive me. Forgive this woman, a holy man's daughter, who prays every day and asks your blessing. I'm usually more careful; I avoid bad words and bad thoughts.'

Now, when I sit beside her, we talk for a few minutes, then lapse into silence. She dozes a little. I clear my throat to wake her up. She opens her eyes and forgets we'd been chatting. She asks after the children again, what I do, where I live and when the family will all be together. She goes back to sleep. I watch her, suppressing enormous sadness. Mother's withdrawing. She's dying a little. I watch her chest rising and falling. I know her heart could give out at any moment, perhaps while she's asleep. She's often spoken of that gentle way of dying. One of her cousins died after the evening prayer. In the morning, she didn't wake up. My mother says she was a good and virtuous woman. God called her to Him in the silence of the night, without making her suffer. Saying that, she's expressing her wish to go the same way. My grandmother died in her sleep too. She was very old. Her funeral was more like a celebration, a party.

Pain and disease are worming their way into her body: the moment of death, the slowness of time and things. That's what my mother fears most. She says that all things come from God. 'It is His will. I'm just a weak little thing in His great light. I pray, I recite God's verses, the words of His holy

Prophet. I wait patiently but I can't bear the suffering. My skin hurts all over; my limbs ache. And I'm bored.'

Boredom, that's the real enemy. God has nothing to do with it. Mother's bored because she doesn't know how to read or write. Again I think of Roland's mother, ninety-two years old and never misses a game of bridge. Last year, she fainted at the foot of the Pyramids. It was the heat and the sudden emotion. But she's still reading and she watches some television programmes. The next day she phones her son to discuss them with him. But Roland goes to bed very early and doesn't watch arts programmes, which are on late. His mother reproaches him for it and secretly laughs at him.

One day I told my mother all the things my friend's mother does at ninety plus. She wasn't surprised: 'That's normal. Those people know how to live. They haven't spent their lives in kitchens and washhouses. We never used to have machines at home. I'd do everything by hand. I had help, but I'd often end up with women who knew less than I did and they'd get on my nerves. Your friend's mother must have had the wherewithal to live comfortably. But we were always hard up. Your father had no commercial sense, yet he kept rushing into bad business ventures. He always said that next time it would work out. We'd get by on just the essentials.'

Perhaps Roland's mother had known other difficulties. My mother never looked at another man. Nor did my sister or my aunt. That's just how it was, a question of habit and of upbringing too. In her family, you married for life.

You didn't divorce. You didn't remarry. The wife of one of my father's friends was caught in bed with her lover. She was repudiated, sent away without a cent. My mother was horrified by this adulterous woman's audacity. She spoke of her pityingly. She couldn't comprehend what she had done or the risks she had taken. It was beyond her.

Roland believes that relations with one's parents are bound to have conflicts. He speaks warmly of his mother, but writes about her with an acuity that borders on malice. Describing the time he visited her at the Résidence de Rumine in Lausanne, he wrote: 'There, a crabby, temperamental old biddy treats me as if my sole purpose in life is to be endlessly at her beck and call. She orders me to phone her friends. They must know that her beloved son has finally come to pay her a visit.' He sees himself as a 'hypocritical son', 'cruel when he writes', but 'kind in day-to-day life'.

It is true that 'blood ties corrupt everything'. But we agree to play the game even to the point of accepting this nasty side of ourselves. I haven't felt the need to be hypocritical, or cynical and cruel. My mother's disarming. Her gaze, her implicit emotional blackmail, her increasingly nebulous demands don't make me feel sadness or compassion but fill me with irrational, selfless love.

As a keen reader of Nietzsche, I'm sometimes shocked by his tumultuous relationships with his sister and his mother. He says he regretted developing the concept of 'eternal recurrence' because it might allow those 'infernal machines' to come back. It's easy to imagine Nietzsche, born of an unknown mother, living with no family, alone on his mountain peak, the image of Zarathustra. But when he was annoyed with his mother, he'd write letters asking for the sausages she used to cook for him when he was a child!

I don't write to my mother. I speak to her. I can no longer ask her to make me a plate of lentils or broad beans in olive oil the way she used to, some years ago.

My mother's become 'crabby and temperamental' too. Illness, boredom and loneliness have brought out the worst in her. She's not a tyrant, but does enjoy exerting her authority over Keltum. She insists she's in charge, constantly repeats herself and exhausts everyone around her. Sometimes she realises what she's doing and asks us not to take any notice of these 'little things'.

16

These 'little things' are becoming more and more of a problem. She'd like someone to come and cut her toenails: Keltum bought some blunt nail-clippers. She'd like Keltum to scratch her back without rushing or nagging her, to be able to go to the bathroom without having to lean on her arm. She'd like to have money on her, to throw down the toilet. She'd like to find her jewellery and wear it as if it were a festive occasion, to go out, walk and even run.

My mother hasn't fasted for over twenty years. The doctors had a hard job persuading her not to keep Ramadan back then. She feels guilty and says that she'll repay her debt to God when she's better. She asks me what I do in France during Ramadan. I explain that the religious and spiritual atmosphere in France isn't conducive to fasting and I don't always observe the strict rules involved. She doesn't take offence or reprimand me, but says: 'That's between you and God.' I love this tolerance.

My parents never forced us to be observant. I remember the harsh winters in Fez. We had to get up early to go and fetch water from the well. Washing with freezing water was an ordeal, and I dreaded those cold mornings. One day, my father summoned my brother and me and said: 'Prayer is one of the five pillars of Islam. You must pray five times a day. You can even say all five at the end of the day. It's not a punishment. If you don't feel the need to pray, then don't pray. But don't pretend, there's no point. On the day of the Last Judgement, you will be alone with your conscience before God. You'll be answerable to the Supreme Being for your actions. It's up to you to decide. I'll never force you to believe. I've done my duty in showing you the path. Besides, Islam is straightforward: to be a good Muslim, it's enough to believe in the one and only God and His Prophet Muhammad, the last of the divine prophets, to behave decently, respecting your parents and the elderly, and not to lie, steal, kill, or hurt others deliberately. As for the rest, it's your choice whether to pray, fast and go to Mecca – those are all external manifestations. Take me, for example: I have no desire to go to Mecca to be exploited by unscrupulous Saudis or trampled on by African giants. And yet I'm a Muslim and have no reason to reproach myself. It's up to you. There are no obligations in Islam, the Prophet himself said so. Do as your conscience dictates.'

Those words, uttered matter-of-factly, were a liberation. I'll never be able to thank my father enough for treating me like an adult. I must have been seven or eight years old. We were still in Fez. My mother wasn't aware of what my father had said to us. But she was equally tolerant.

I'm not sure where it comes from, but anxiety is a given in our family. It's been passed on from generation to generation. Dread, the idea of loss, fear of an accident ... our life's been beset by worry. I can't think which of my parents was the most apprehensive. I think my father transmitted the habit to my mother. Still today, if I'm an hour late for lunch, my mother has palpitations and turns pale. She instantly imagines the worst. When she was well, she'd sit by the window and wait. Sometimes she'd throw on a djellaba and go out into the street, hoping to make me come more quickly. All Mediterranean mothers are anxious creatures. Mine must be a little more so than others. I couldn't stand her excessive shows of affection. I'd be irritated, I'd protest, and afterwards be angry with myself. I was ashamed to have hurt my poor mother. She'd be relieved and say: 'When you have children, you'll see. Your heart won't be able to stand what mine's already had to bear!' Then, when she was calm again, she'd add: 'I know it annoys you, but it's the way God made me. He's the one who gave me such a sensitive soul. There's nothing I can do, I don't think I'll ever change. If one of my children's away from home, if I don't know where they are or what they're doing, I can't sleep. That's just the way it is; my heart goes wild, half-crazy; there's no logic to it. It beats louder when I think of you. Life's so unpredictable, so full of accidents, you must try to understand. You'll see in time!'

In time, I've neither understood nor accepted this stifling affection. I try not to replicate this behaviour with my own children. But I confess that my parents have passed on their tendency to fret and worry.

I was sixteen when I attended my first political meeting. We'd met at a friend's house to form a high-school students' union to fight repression in Morocco. I'd come home at about two o'clock in the morning. My parents were on the doorstep, my father threatening, my mother in tears. Before my father started on me, I kissed my mother's hand and asked her forgiveness: 'I was at a meeting. We're going to organise strikes to stop the police beating us up!' My parents were alarmed. 'No more meetings! No more politics!' yelled my father. He knew what the Moroccan police were like. One summer, while we were on holiday staying with my cousins in Casablanca, our house was burgled. My father, in a calm and determined voice, asked us not to touch anything. The police had to come and take fingerprints, make a report. Our poor father! He thought he was in an American cop film. The police turned up and took him away in a van. He was ashamed: all the neighbours came out to watch the scene. The police treated him as if he were the thief. At the police station, he'd been left to wait in a corridor. Many hours later, he was interrogated, like a hooligan. They quizzed him relentlessly about his children, his business and his habits.

In the end he stood up and said, with typically mordant humour that was completely lost on the police: 'I'm sorry, gentlemen, I swear I won't do it again, this is the very last time. Now let me go.'

So in the end we didn't file a complaint and my father said to us solemnly: 'In this country, it's the plaintiff, the person that's been attacked and robbed, who's judged, not the thief, who shares the spoils with his police pals. Make sure you never fall into their hands. They're people with no principles, no education. That's how it is here, this isn't Sweden!'

Later, when my parents heard about my political meeting, they saw the spectre of the police descending on the house.

That scene was to determine later events. My mother dates the beginning of her high blood pressure and her diabetes from that time. The dawn arrival of a jeep from the gendarmerie that would convey me to an army disciplinary camp was traumatic for her. I was twenty-two, and still a student. The eighteen months I spent in camp aggravated her condition. Even though she believes that it was written, she still says God might have spared her that. Her failing memory confuses that episode with other unhappy events. But she does remember that her son was taken away from her for several months. She muddles up months and years. 'The police. Yes, son, those brutes ruined my health. You said it was nothing serious, but they had a murderous look in their eyes. You went away, and I didn't know what to do with myself. I paced the house like a madwoman. The truth is, I went crazy, and so did your father. We had no information. I thought of you, I knew you wouldn't cope with the hunger and the injustice. But God alone dispenses justice. I thought of our neighbour's son Miloud, the poor boy – they took him off in a jeep and his parents never saw him again. The police told them: "Your son ran away; he's probably living in Algeria or Spain. Must have a guilty conscience." His parents fell ill and their son never came back.'

I don't remember ever complimenting my mother, either on her cooking or her appearance. She'd often chide us for it, especially at mealtimes. She'd have liked to hear kind words, such as: 'May God give you health and keep you, so your hands continue to feed us so well!' Or: 'You're the best cook in the world.'

When my brother and I were invited to my uncle's or to friends', my mother insisted on knowing every detail of what we'd eaten and our opinion of the food. That was the way she fished for compliments. We were fairly sparing when it came to tender or loving words. That was the general rule: you didn't show your feelings in public, or express them. Above all, you avoided any display of affection. I don't remember hearing my father or mother ever talk about love. You don't say 'I love you', you don't kiss in public, you don't parade your private life in front of your children. Modesty and respect are all.

17

I haven't seen my mother for a month. To her, that's a small eternity. She said as much yesterday, on the phone: 'You don't realise, but you haven't been to see me in such a long time. I'm going to die without having seen your children again. I know they've grown up but tell me, does your eldest daughter live with you or has she moved out? When are you coming? After Ramadan? My God, that's such a long time! No, come before, just a little, I'm dying of this love. I know because it's so painful. And I'm bored. I have nothing to do, I'm just here, stuck in a corner like a bag of bones that doesn't move. Your poor mother's mad, is what you're thinking. Go on, say it, it doesn't worry me. It's true in a way – not all the time, but sometimes I lose track of time and get everything muddled. Pills aren't always your friends; they're deceptive, they help and they harm. Half the time they heal, the other half they attack. So, when are you coming? Tomorrow? No? Why not, son? You're so far away, you can't, you have too much work. Now, where is it you work? You've told me but I forget. Forgetting is the enemy. Your father used to say I had the forgetting disease. He'd say it to annoy me. He'd ask me to remind him what we'd had for supper the night before, and I couldn't always remember everything. You want my blessing? But you already have it, you and your brothers and sister, you have all my blessing. You need more, I know, because you're in the public eye. You attract so much jealousy and envy. People are spiteful; they don't like successful people, they put the evil eye on them. But I'm watching out, making sure God protects you and shields you from all their scheming and mischief-making. I know and my heart can see black shadows swooping round you like vultures; they want to hurt you. But I know they're wasting their time, you're the grandson of a saint, they can't touch you. Let them get all worked up, you're better than them. I don't know about spite myself; I've never been nasty to anyone. That's how it is, it's just my nature, I couldn't even think of hurting anyone, but some people have a talent for it. You need to know that, and watch out, but when you're good you don't need to watch out. I was just saying that to my father. You know, he came back and his beard was all white, he put his arms around me and whispered in my ear. The house is full of guests, I wonder why they're all here. I'm telling you: be wary of people, the ones who try to take advantage of you. They won't succeed. Go, son, don't forget the wishes I send with you; they're all wholesome and good, you deserve them. But be careful. God has given you a gift; your fingers are precious. Whatever you touch, you'll be blessed. Stone will turn to gold, gold to love, and you, who are so good and simple, you're my son, the one who loves me so much! My father's going, he left with our Prophet. Fez is a marvellous city at the moment. Tangier? Where is that? No, I'm telling you: I'm in Fez with my parents, and I'm playing with all the boxes of pills Sidi Mohammed left behind. You know he died, poor man, he died and never even saw his daughter …'

That still upsets my brothers, they know the youngest is often spoilt. When we were children, she treated us all equally. She loved us with the same fervour. In the mornings, before sending us to school, she'd slip ten raisins into each of our pockets, saying: 'It's to make you clever! They say that a plump raisin nourishes the mind, so if you eat them every morning, you'll never be stupid. In any case, my children are never naughty. And besides, the monkey loves her little ones, however ugly they are. I love you and you are handsome. Go in God's light and do well, so you pass all your exams.'

When we came home from school, we'd shout: 'We're hungry!' before we even reached the door. Mother did her utmost to stop us shouting in the street. She was convinced the neighbours would be saying things like: 'That family starves the children, she doesn't give them enough to eat, those people are either mean or poor.' The neighbours said no such thing because their own children were shouting the same as us. But my mother was careful to be discreet. That's probably why she never raises her voice. She never shouts.

She doesn't like strong colours or perfumes. She loves brightness, light, open spaces. She says that light makes the heart swell, deep brown darkens the horizon, black cuts us off from life, noise distances us from people, panic invites death, sleeplessness puts darkness deep in the eyes, money's the dirt of life. God fills our heart with His presence and His light wards off evil. 'If you buy me a headscarf, choose one with the colours of a sunny springtime. I don't want black, I've never worn black.'

18

Today she's wearing a white *tchamir*, a kind of long robe that serves as a nightdress. She doesn't like this *tchamir*. She asks for her beautiful caftans, her *mansourias* and her headscarves. 'I'm not taking them to the grave with me, I'd rather wear them now than never.' Keltum says: 'I'll give them to you after you've had your bath.' And then forgets.

Mother doesn't like herself any more. She no longer wants to look in a mirror. She adjusts the scarf on her head and sighs as if she were condemned never to get dressed again. I hold out the little mirror she keeps in her handbag. She looks away, then slowly turns towards the mirror, seeking her reflection, and then hangs her head as if she's about to cry. I put the mirror back in the bag. She starts to complain, while Keltum rolls her eyes at me to signal she's off again. I know she's thrown bank notes and jewellery down the toilet countless times, I know she rips her *tchamir* and refuses to wear incontinence pads. She won't talk to me about it. Even in her delusions, she's well-mannered, reserved and modest. She complains too much. Nothing new about that. It's a way of passing the time, of having something to say.

The other day, as I kissed her hand, she held on to mine and brought it to her lips to kiss. At first I resist, then let her have her way. She keeps it in hers. Even her hands are tiny now. She speaks in a slow, soft voice: 'I'm a beggar woman; I pick up the dead leaves of time, one day here, one week there. I've been gathering up the hours for a long time and putting them over there in the corner of the room. Don't you think the room's got narrower? It's like a grave. Maybe that's what death is. My room will cave in, the walls around me will close in and bury me. I was telling you I'm the beggar of time, but sometimes I no longer want to take the time God gives. I'm not picking up anything any more. I bend over and there are no more hours lying around. My eyesight's got worse. I can't see things or hours any more. I can see them but they're blurry and faraway, they look strange. That's boredom for you; it's deceiving me, lying to me, making the days look as if they shimmer with light and splendour, and in fact they're nothing like that. I'm not a young girl any more, for it to tease me like that. You see, son, I say whatever comes into my head and then I forget all about it. But tell me: yesterday was the start of Ramadan and I'm not fasting, the doctor forbade it. But I'm praying, and asking God for forgiveness. Although I'm not eating much, I'm not very hungry. Don't forget to buy the sheep for Eid.'

She's confusing Eid al-Fitr, the festival that marks the end of Ramadan, with Eid al-Adha, the festival of the sacrifice that takes place seventy days later. Of course, I'll buy a sheep and we'll give the meat to the poor. Keltum looks at me as if afflicted. She'll have her mutton to eat with her children.

I usually give my mother a copy of each book I publish. I bring it to her, put it in her hands and summarise the story for her. She opens it, leafs through, either the right way round or back to front, then says a prayer to bless it. She often starts an argument over some detail. For her, a book is the truth. Facts must not be twisted.

The other day, she had a visit from one of her nieces, Sumaya, who's married to a billionaire. This woman once phoned me to lecture me on literature: 'Stop writing books that aren't at all Moroccan, that treat our religion irreverently. God will punish you because you take liberties with our beautiful religion. You should dedicate your pen to the service of Islam and the Muslim nation and stop writing stories that are of no interest to Morocco, books for the Christians. You're betraying your country and your religion, and what's worse, you don't even write in Arabic. You should start learning the language of the Qur'an and devote yourself to good causes – just causes, which defend Islam and banish infidels. You paint a negative picture of our country, you ought to be ashamed ...' etc.

This girl, who was married off very young by my uncle because she was such a hussy, now goes around proselytising. Every time she visits my mother, she gives her a bound copy of the Qur'an and asks her to urge me to change the subject of my novels. My mother says she'll be sure to pass on the message. 'You know, son, your cousin Sumaya gave me another holy book. Look, it's beautiful. You ought to write a book like this one. She's right; if you write a book like this, you'll be a holy man, and your enemies won't be able to say a word!'

Write the Qur'an! I don't know whether mother's joking or delusional. 'Yemma, the Qur'an is the Word of God, no one can rewrite it or say they have written it. It's a miracle book, unique, sacred and eternal, how can your son compete with God?'

'Ask God for forgiveness, son! I didn't suggest you write the Qur'an, but a book in the same spirit. That's what Sumaya's asking, and she's right. But do what you want to do, you're a grown man and responsible. You know, sometimes I'm afraid of the people who want to hurt you. They're jealous, their eyes bore holes in whatever they look at. They're bad people, and you should watch out for the ones who say they're your friends. It's the people close to you who can do you the most harm; the ones further away, who hardly know you, can't hurt you. They can talk, but no one will necessarily believe them. The ones who know you are more credible. You're too trusting, you should be careful: success is like a very bright light, it dazzles the people in front of you, it makes them weak and resentful, jealous and covetous. And the worst of it is that they put the evil eye on you. They think you don't deserve success. But God has placed you above those who want to harm you. Believe me, I know what I'm talking about. My father was a saint – light radiated from his face. He's the one who taught me that natural goodness is a gift from God. I am good, I've never wanted to hurt anyone, even the people who are jealous of you, I leave them to God. You know, your father wasn't always kind – he envied shopkeepers who did well. I often told him to stop being jealous. He would curse and shout but he had no defence. I saw him yesterday, you know, he came to visit me. He was wearing a white djellaba and a bright red tarbouche, and he smelled of paradise. He was smiling. He's got younger.'

'But Yemma, Father died more than ten years ago!'

'Oh, I see, he died and no one told me! In any case, I saw him. Death suits him: his skin was clear and his eyes were calm. Death puts things in their place. His soul is travelling. That's it – it was his soul I saw. It smelled good. You know your father never dressed well, he always wore those dark-brown djellabas I hated. He didn't like changing his shirt every day, he said that appearances didn't matter. He was clean, but he didn't care for fine clothes. Luckily you're not like him. You dress very well. That annoys people too, they can't bear other people looking good. Envy ... It's incredible how jealous people can be. I worry when I see you on television because your image is everywhere, it goes into every house. I don't like you being on television too much, being seen so much, it all stirs up your enemies' hatred, and they start spreading gossip the moment your back is turned.

They all want to be in your shoes. Watch out for the ones who are always smiling at you, the ones who flatter you and tell you you're the best. They're the ones who'll ambush you, son – like your father's friend, that businessman who claimed to be juggling millions – you know, the one who got your father to hand over all his savings, which he put in a fake bank account, and your father never got the money back – that one. I've prayed to God to punish him and keep him away from trusting people so he can't steal from them any more. Watch out! Wait, I can't see anything, where are my glasses? It's all gone dark. Help me look, maybe I dropped them. Look under the bed …'

'But Yemma, you're wearing them, it's a power cut. The light will come back on soon. Take my hand and we'll pray together for the light to come back!'

'What was I saying? Remind me what I was talking about. I can't remember recent things, but I remember old things very clearly. It's strange, the oldest memories are the most faithful, they don't leave me, whereas this morning's, I didn't keep them, I don't know what I did with them. Maybe they fell on the floor, like the glasses. Old memories stay with us till the grave. What happens to them afterwards? I have no idea. Sometimes I imagine a big shop, a kind of warehouse that the dead pass through before they're buried, where they leave their old memories and then go off to the house of God, feeling lighter. I can't wait to go there. I mean it, I'm tired, I'm worn out, and I can't bear these two women skulking around. They look at me with hyena eyes.

They're waiting for me to go, so they can take all my things. I can read their expressions, I learn things even when they don't say anything. You remember our neighbours, the old French couple? The husband died first. Their housekeeper took advantage of the wife's illness to steal everything from her. She even had a lorry come to take it all away. The next day, we found out that the old woman had died. In fact, she'd died very early that morning. The housekeeper didn't tell anyone, she used that time to clear the place out. The police came and the housekeeper made a deal with them. I'm scared those two will steal everything I have left. That's why we have to watch out. I know possessions aren't important to you. You say we shouldn't get attached to things, but they're all I have, and I don't want anyone to steal from me, either now or after I die. Get a pencil and a piece of paper and write down: seven caftans embroidered in the seven colours I love: white, beige, pale yellow, sky blue, mauve, light green, pink, midnight blue, off-white …'

'But Yemma, that's more than seven …'

'It doesn't matter. The main thing is that I have a dozen caftans, some of them are still brand-new. Put down two headscarves for each outfit, matching of course, five *mansourias*, and four belts embroidered in Fez by Maître Bennis … Then the djellabas for special occasions; I'm leaving out the everyday djellabas, they're nothing special. So, there are five silk djellabas sewn by Maître Bennis' son. Don't forget the embroidered handkerchiefs I have for parties and ceremonies. There's no point putting down underwear and pyjamas. Write the list of my jewellery in your notebook, after the clothes …'

'But Yemma, you've already given your jewellery to your granddaughters and their mother. You've got no jewellery left, or very little.'

'Is that right? I don't have any more jewellery! Didn't I tell you, I'm surrounded by enemies and thieves? My jewellery's been stolen – that's it, Keltum and that fat woman took it while I was sleeping or when I was in the hospital.'

'No, Yemma, you gave it to me to look after and then I shared it out according to your instructions.'

'Are you sure? Or are you saying that to keep me quiet? Well anyway, it doesn't matter. Let's say the jewellery's disappeared. Put down the other things I own: the sitting room, more particularly the wool in the sitting-room mattresses: it's wool I bought in Fez with my savings; your father refused to do up the house. There's a tonne of it – no, less, maybe 400 kilos – you should take it for your house. It's very good quality, pure wool, which makes mattresses very comfortable. Then there's the carpets, the Rabat one as well as the one from Fez. They're old, and very good quality. Don't sell them off cheap. Also the tea service, which was made in London, you have to look after it …'

'But Yemma, you gave that tea set to my brother on his wedding day, thirty years ago …'

'Write it down, I say, don't try to confuse me. I'm not mad. I'm well aware your brother has the tea service, but that's no reason not to make a note of it, we can sort it out later … I don't care about the TV – or the radio, it hasn't worked in twenty years, but your father liked to keep everything: keys and broken locks, batteries, clapped-out lamps, everything, and the radio's part of the job lot, it's furniture … Ah, the curtains! I hate them. Do me a favour, take them down and give them to Keltum, she'll know what to do with them. The old wardrobe's heavy and cumbersome, it should stay where it is, it's useful for storing food. It's got woodworm and the doors don't close, but it's part of the house. The mirror, the huge one in the corridor, is tarnished. Take it for your house. Your father loved it, but I don't know what to do with it. It's so high up, and I've shrunk, I can't see myself in it, so it's no use. You know your cousin, the one who lost his wife last year, he's over eighty and he's just remarried. He was broken by loneliness – he told me that the other day. We're quite close because we're the same generation. He's found a woman from a good family, she's in her fifties, but his children have taken it very badly – that's how it is, they loved their mother and can't bear another woman to take her place; and of course the wife will have her share of the inheritance, too … You know, towards the end of his life, your father tried to take another wife, a young one, like the girl who came to give him his injections. But I wouldn't have it – over my dead body, I told him. When I'm gone, you can marry whoever you like. Sort it out with your children. But while I still have breath, I won't allow you to do something so disastrous. I wasn't jealous, but I can't bear the lack of respect. I have my dignity, my honour. So he gave up the idea … When he comes, later on, ask him to tell you about it. It was while you were studying in France. You weren't living with us – you'd come to see us in the summer, then disappear for the rest of the year.'

'But Yemma, Father's dead, have you forgotten again?'

'No I haven't forgotten, but the dead visit us from time to time, we shouldn't shut the door in their faces. It's not right, and it brings bad luck. The dead are like angels, they pass by, leave a lingering scent and are gone. Your father often comes to see what's going on in the house. He's not always happy, he grumbles, but since the dead don't speak, I hear sighs coming from somewhere. You know, after my death I'll come back too. Be mindful, always leave a window open, don't keep everything closed. In any case, the soul can pass through walls and forests, it makes its way even into your sleep, into your dreams, makes them more real, more vivid. I'm not scared of death, no, not scared at all. It's God's will, and anyway to die is to meet the saints, with our Prophet and with God. So I have nothing to fear, quite the opposite, I'm delighted. It's other people dying that scares me. I don't like seeing cold, stiff bodies, and I don't like sleeping in the room where the dead have been washed. That's how it is, the strange smells of the soulless body, the whiteness of the shroud, the date halves on the face. That whole ritual offends my eyes. I'm not hungry, I'm not sleepy, my water's leaked out. How shaming. Yes, I've wet myself, like a child. You see, your mother's turned into a little thing that can't control itself. I say whatever comes into my head, I mix up all my

103

memories and I get confused about time. But I still have my mind. Lapses: yes, I have memory lapses. Even people who are well have memory lapses. You understand, little brother. You remember when we were playing in the neighbours' garden in Fez? You'd get caught and I'd hide. Come to think of it, it's been a long time since you came to see me. I'm your older sister, you have a duty to your older sister, don't you? Or is it your wife stopping you from going out?'

'But Yemma, I'm not your little brother, I'm your son, your last child, I'm fifty-six and I'm alive. Your little brother died twenty years ago, and so did his wife.'

19

In the summer of 1953, the Fez medina was silent and lifeless. The shopkeepers were on strike. Political rallies were held in the mosques, followed by demonstrations demanding independence. Morocco couldn't live without Mohammed V, who'd been deposed by the French and exiled to Madagascar. The face of Fez was changing, and so was its fate. People spoke of resistance and armed struggle. All commercial activity was to cease as a sign of protest. Some people took advantage of the situation, trading on the black market and then turning police informant. Shopkeepers and craftsmen came together in an effort to bring France to its knees. I remember a meeting at the house of my aunt's husband. Allal El Fassi, the party leader, arrived, surrounded by his supporters. My sister's husband was there too, a potter, a very humble and brave man. I heard them say our country was in danger. They spoke of freedom, the Istiqlal party, independence. My uncle had confiscated one of my toys, a spinning top. He'd even hurt me, by tugging my ear: 'You think this is a time to play and have fun? The country's rising up and you're playing spinning tops!' I couldn't see how my top was going to hinder the country's liberation. The streets were deserted. Fez wasn't the same. The city had been shrouded in a crumpled sheet, no longer allowed to celebrate; there was no joy or even light. It was decaying even as it became the centre of Moroccan nationalism. All I knew was that my father was unhappy, torn between his urge to fight the French and the determination not to lose his business. After a month of striking and demonstrating, he could no longer feed his family.

'Fez! Oh my husband, my young husband!' she says suddenly. 'Fez, city of cities, the most beautiful of cities, city of civilisation, home of the Muslim religion, morality and good family. Oh my husband! What a mistake it was to leave Fez. But everyone left. Its people – the ones with roots there and ancestors in El Guebeb, the most beautiful cemetery in the world – betrayed it. They went to Casablanca to make their fortunes! You're right to regret the move. You and your business were doing badly, so one evening you came home and said: "Wife, we're going to Tangier. My brother's made me an offer to start up a business. There's nothing here any more, nothing's working. Since our king was exiled, it's been a disaster." I said: "Wait a little, the king will come back and business will pick up." You shouted at me: "You can't give me advice!" I followed you in silence, as usual, I agreed because

I had no choice, and there was my other son, of course, the one you never accepted, the son I had with my first husband. The first or the second? I don't know any more. Anyway he wasn't yours. He came with us to help you, but it all went wrong. And there I was, far from Fez, far from the most beautiful cemetery in the world, far from Moulay Idriss, the city's saint. And alone. I'm talking to myself, but who are you, smiling at me? Oh, you came back! But why don't you say anything? You've grown younger, your skin's soft, your wrinkles are gone. But so have your eyes. What are those white balls in place of your eyes? Answer me! Say something! You're usually so talkative, you used to talk all the time and never let me get a word in. Well, I'm going to make the most of it, I'm going to tell you everything that's been bothering me for such a very long time. Listen carefully: I'm not a bad person, I don't gossip. I have a tendency to moan a bit, to complain, like children do. But now I'm going to speak to you with the respect a wife owes her husband. I haven't been happy with you, the sun never shone when I was with you, you never called me by my name, you couldn't say Lalla Fatma, or even Fatma. I would have been happy with just my name, and you can leave the Lalla to the princesses! I was short of money all the time. I know you didn't have much, but you were stingy. I'm sorry if I sound brutal, but I feel I have a duty to tell you everything. Maybe stingy isn't the right word. You were thrifty, afraid of not having enough, and of having to borrow from your brother, who was rich but even stingier than you. You never made

107

your fortune. We didn't go without, we just had the bare minimum. We weren't starving but I didn't have enough to buy caftans or jewellery. If there was a party, I'd ask my little sister if I could borrow her things. I'd cry and you'd just look nervous, putting your hand to your forehead, which was hot because you suffered from migraines. You didn't even look at me. I was your wife and your servant too. You liked being waited on and I'd kiss your right hand the way I used to kiss my father's. You liked that submissiveness, but you weren't tender towards me. When I saw how my brothers and sister lived with their spouses, I couldn't help my eyes filling with tears, thinking of my situation. Tell me the truth today: did you love me? You never showed the least sign of affection. When I talked about our life together, you'd be embarrassed, you always changed the subject. You liked entertaining and making jokes about people who weren't there. It wasn't very kind, but my family liked your wit, your irony. You made them laugh, but you never made me laugh. I'd have loved it if you'd made me laugh, had fun with me, making jokes … Oh, I know you said I didn't understand your sense of humour, that it went over my head … Now that we're nearly equal, you in the cemetery and me lying on this bed, waiting for death, we can tell each other everything. But you can't talk any more, you're just an apparition, a fine figure of a man, good-looking. And me wittering on. Give me something to drink – no, not milk, water; you know I can't take milk in the mornings. Thank you. Help me to sit up or I might choke on it and that hurts. How many times you nearly died from drinking too fast, a gulp of water going down the wrong way. Panic and impatience run in the family. You want everything right now. No, husband. I'm being careful, I'm going to drink slowly. So, will you hurry up?'

'I'm coming, Yemma, take your pill with it, it's for your blood pressure, yes, your blood pressure's high, like your son's, the blood's pressing the arteries, we have to lower it.'

'All right, my love! I'm tired, I'm waiting. Yes, you at least I can tell: I'm waiting for the last goodbye. You're my son, aren't you? Your father was here just now, he came to see if I was ready. I forgot to tell him I was tired and longing to join him. I made a mess of it, all I did was blame him, I told him what was on my mind, but you I can tell: I've had enough of waiting, it's as if I'd been left on a station platform and I'm waiting for the train. But I have a feeling the station's closed down, there are no more trains coming through, it's covered in weeds, it's cold, there are draughts. Strange people are passing by and then they fall over. No one comes to help, they're just left there. It's definitely a station because I can see the rails. There's even a lone carriage, abandoned on the track. I think it's turned into a refuge for the poor, for people who have nowhere to stay. But I'm in my house, what can I do, I'm stuck here, staring at the wall opposite. The wall's just a pile of stones, it doesn't answer me, it's not a mirror. I watch everything around me and I think of the future. Oh, not my grandchildren's wide-open future, but my own. Leaving you, not being a burden on you any more. I know you're patient, you don't get annoyed, you're here because you love me and the love I have for you fills my heart and spills over. That's simply the way it is, I didn't choose it, but when I think of you, my heart beats faster and fills with love till it drowns. Yes, my love is a flood. I'm sorry, I know that's a burden, you've already told me that. I'm here waiting and I see the magnificent light, it's our Prophet's face, a dazzling light. That's what death is, we depart on the rays of that light, we no longer suffer, we're calm. Just thinking about it makes me feel better, less anxious. I'm feeling a little sleepy now, I might take a nap. Perhaps I won't wake up, like my mother. She went in her sleep. She was still all there, she wasn't crazy like me. You know I … Don't pretend to reassure me. I just said your father was here. Well, that's crazy. Your father died ten years, two months and three days ago! The dead don't travel, but maybe what I see doesn't exist. That's what it is, I have visions, like sick people who get feverish. I see things that aren't there, I talk to ghosts, to apparitions. Oh dear me no, your father wouldn't have liked being called an apparition, and especially not a ghost. No, I'm making things up – it's because of the deserted station and the pills, especially the ones that make me feel drowsy, sluggish and strange. They settle my nerves and send me off on journeys … When I go wandering, I'm not afraid of anything. I forget my pain and just walk. You see, son, that's how we go and don't come back. But you have to be there, with your brothers and sister. It's important – for me and for you, because once I'm dead you'll forget me. That's how it is. You'll have an image of me that's calm and serene. Give alms

110

on Fridays, give to the poor, recite a few verses from the Qu'ran at my grave. I know you don't like going to graves; well then, don't come. I know I'm in your heart and I won't need you in the cemetery. I didn't go to my parents' graves much either, they're buried in … I can't remember if they're buried here in Fez or over there in Tangier. But where am I? Remind me where we are. That woman's shouting "Tangier" from the kitchen. She's listening to our conversation, she must be working with the police, but I'm not afraid any more. So what was I talking about, my stolen jewels or your son's circumcision? You must circumcise him or he won't be Muslim … I'm talking too much. It's the emptiness making me talk. When you're here, I talk all the time. I tell you the same story for the hundredth time. I repeat myself. Yes, I say the same things again and again. Forgive me, son, you understand. The others don't. My daughter gets upset and tells me off for repeating the same stories, she says I'm losing my mind. Then she goes off to the kitchen and leaves me all alone. So I go on talking as if she was here. I'm not crazy, I'm just tired.'

20

The other day, my mother asked me why I never visit my father's grave. Because I'm just not able to concentrate on a slab of marble. I read and reread the headstone and my thoughts wander. I prefer to carry his memory inside me, and I dream about him often. Better than that, I think about him and realise I'm becoming more and more like him. I have the same little habits, the same moods and, perhaps, the same rage. Like him, I can't bear insincerity, betrayal, injustice or hypocrisy. 'Neither can I,' said my mother. 'But he went too far. Have you forgotten how he'd lose his temper over nothing, son? Food that was too salty, or a window that didn't close. I put up with his outbursts, I said nothing, I waited for the storm to blow over. But one time he really went too far. You were there, I felt you protecting me, I felt strong. So I told him what I thought of him and his wretched behaviour. He threatened me, I think he raised his arm to hit me. I ran out of the house like a madwoman, with no djellaba on. I couldn't stand it any more. I was outside, with no idea where to go. You came, followed by your brother, and took me back to the house. I remember you'd invited a young woman over, a European, and I felt ashamed. I must admit he never hit me. His tongue hurt more than his hands. He couldn't control his rage or his bitterness. He was unhappy, often jealous of those doing better than him in business. He had a habit of pointing out that such-and-such a millionaire used to be an apprentice in his shop in Fez. I didn't like that resentment. I hope you won't take after him in that respect. My blessing and my prayers will protect you from anyone trying to hurt you. But you never know, people are so fickle. The man who embraces you today will stab you in the back tomorrow. God keep us from wicked people! I must pray for you and your brothers. I have a feeling you need it; I can see the shadows prowling around you. But never fear, you're in God's hands. He is watching you, in my eyes, in my stomach, in my heart. You're in my deepest thoughts, the ones that go from my heart to God the Most High, He who guides our steps and keeps wayward souls away from us: people without scruples, those who take advantage of our goodness and our trust, the ones dissatisfied with life, with heaven, with God. Your heart is pure as silk, you have nothing to fear, God will raise you above those whose eyes are full of envy … Oh dear, I haven't taken my pills. That's one of Keltum's tricks. She wants to get rid of me. She told me yesterday that the pharmacy won't give us credit any more. She has unpaid bills. Can you believe it? The pharmacist can't do that, Keltum's just making it up so as not to give me my pills. She's an ignorant woman. Your father detested ignorance. He said that all evil comes from ignorance. What can we do, my son? You spoke to the pharmacist. That's good, I knew you would. You know, I complain about Keltum but I couldn't bear to see her go. She knows that, so she blackmails me. She makes me cry. She puts on her djellaba and tells me she's leaving. You see how I suffer? She's the only one who knows which pills I take, the only one who can take me to the bathroom. She washes me, but she's not gentle. She often shouts and frightens me. But my own daughter refuses to wash me, so I put up with Keltum's cruelty. Sometimes I say to myself she's my fourth husband – a tyrant, full of anger, never happy, except when you're here and you give her extra on top of her wages. Why don't you move in here, close to me? I'd see you every day and I wouldn't be afraid of the tricks Keltum plays. Why not come and live in this house? It's big, you still have your room. Oh yes, I forgot, you're married and you have children. You live far away. What are your children's names and how many do you have? Let me guess. Oh forgetting, this devilish forgetting, it's the enemy, stealing everything from me. It comes just like that and takes my memories – by what right? Go on, you're educated, why do people forget? So I was telling you your father hadn't come to see me this week and my little brother won't stop his singing in the yard, he doesn't even dare push the door open and come to keep me company. I know his wife's stopping him. Give me a drink, I'm thirsty, and I have to say my prayers. I've already said them? I don't remember. Did you see me pray? That's no good, son, so turn off the TV, come and sit beside me and read the Qur'an. You'd rather it was your elder brother, who knows the Qur'an better than you. But you went to the M'sid, the Qur'anic school in Buajarra in Fez. You've forgotten? No, you can't forget the M'sid and Fqih Meftah, the teacher with only one eye, who saw everything … He was very strict, he always had his stick to wake up the ones who fell asleep. You don't remember Fqih …? What was his name again? Help, I said his name five minutes ago … Fettah … Fellah … Mftuh … Fettuh … F … I saw him yesterday, he brought me a lovely bunch of fresh mint. He's a good man. What's his name? He's going to come by again to give me the coupons, so we can go and get the oil and the flour. Soon the war'll be over. I hope there won't be coupons for food … What, you weren't born in the days of coupons? But of course you were … You were twenty years old and you wanted to marry … What was her name, the girl with the long hair?'

My mother dozed off trying to remember the name of the teacher at the Qur'anic school. She has absences, periods when she's not there, her eyes half-closed, her mouth open, her head lolling. I don't like seeing her like that. She's like a badly assembled object, a thing that doesn't hold together. She lets herself go, collapses and becomes insignificant … my mother is breathing … I watch her chest rise and fall and I wait.

It reminds me of 1977, when she went into Salé hospital for a cataract operation. She had to lie on her back for thirty days with her eyes bandaged. I spent a lot of time with her. We had to watch out, make sure she didn't rip off her dressings. My brother would come in the evening, after work. But I was there all the time, of course. I was free, no boss, no children; a writer's time is his own. I'd talk to her, and she'd tell me family stories, asking me not to write them down, not to name names. At the time, I was writing *Moha the Mad, Moha the Wise* and I was angry. Morocco had become a police state, colluding with people who claimed not to be involved in politics but were shamelessly lining their pockets, making corruption a way of life. I remember times when, driven by fury, one eye on my sleeping mother, the other on my notebook, I'd be anxiously scribbling away. My mother had no idea what I was writing. She could hear the scratching of pen on paper and would say: 'Be careful, I'm afraid for you!' I'd reassure her, then she'd ask whether our neighbours' eldest son had been found, whether his parents had had any news. His disappearance made her agitated. She put herself in his parents' shoes and couldn't understand why a young man who'd done nothing wrong had simply vanished overnight. She didn't mention the king, or his ministers, but said the police were cruel and heartless. She thought about the neighbours' son, Miloud, ripped from his family by police in plain clothes. That's what a police state is: arbitrary punishment, cruelty and brutality. How many mothers have suffered, and doubtless died of grief, because of a police directive to 'disappear' a child of theirs, a child who'd demonstrated in favour of justice and democracy! Morocco has known dark years, when all opposition was suppressed – even the most common, non-violent kind: ideas.

'Keep away from politics, son, stay out of it. You know they tried to kill the king, they killed so many people during his birthday celebrations, but fortunately God protected him. They started again the year after. I remember it clearly, we were all so afraid. If they'd managed to murder him, they'd have murdered us too. I know we're not involved in politics but you, you were punished. There's no arguing with army people. What a time that was: fear, fear everywhere. Beggars and servants spying on families, everyone suspicious of everyone else. Do you remember that customer of your father's who was arrested and put in prison because his brother was in the army and had, I think, taken part in the killing? The whole family was punished. God preserve us from the army and its methods!'

She vividly remembers that period. The ordeal of the eye operation is not easily forgotten. She still talks about it: 'It was so painful, especially lying on my back, not moving, in the dark. Not being able to lift my head. I remember. You were there, you were writing, and I was thinking of poor Miloud, who'd disappeared, Your father was complaining because he'd stayed in Tangier on his own. I thought of him and I have to admit that not seeing him for a month was a

117

relief. Marriage, son, is also a habit you get used to, it can be a chore or a torment. I was thinking of my health, he was ranting because the maid wasn't as good a cook as me – a funny way to compliment me on my cooking! Anyway, that's all in the past. And whatever happened to your book? Hand me my glasses, I'm going to watch TV. It's Friday, they should be showing midday prayers.'

'But Yemma, it's Monday and TV's not broadcasting prayers but a Mexican soap where everyone speaks classical Arabic.'

'I know my sight's getting worse, but my hearing's excellent. I can hear the Qur'an, can't I? Isn't that the Qur'an they're reading?'

'No, Yemma, no one's reading the Qur'an, it's in your head, you can hear prayers in the distance ...'

'Then my time must be near. We must get the sitting room in order and invite the *tolba* to read the Qur'an over my body. I'm sure to go in the daytime – you should be ready. I want a wonderful party with the city's best *tolba*, reading and singing the beautiful words of God. I want them to be well looked-after and well paid, I want them to leave feeling happy and contented. We must feed them – maybe we should book a caterer. Apparently it's quicker and more efficient. These days caterers solve all our problems, especially at funerals. Can you believe it: misfortune strikes and people don't have the generosity or the time to make a meal for all the visitors who pour in from other cities to offer their condolences? So, first the caterer, then reading the words of

God. Don't forget the paradise incense. Come closer. I have to tell you, I put some aside and hid it, especially for that day. You should know where I've hidden it, where … Oh, I can't remember – what a disaster. To think my memory lets me down just when I need it the most. It's an incense my daughter brought me back from Mecca. It's extraordinary, very strong, very fragrant, it's sublime. But I can't remember the hiding place! You'll have to look for it. Don't ask Keltum, she'll just steal it. Go and rummage around in the wardrobe, in the drawers, it's in a white handkerchief. My God, help me remember …'

'But Yemma, I'll buy you some … the main thing is to have the paradise incense. Don't worry, you'll have a lovely funeral, I promise, my brothers and I will make sure of it, you can sleep in peace.'

Whenever my mother gets bored, she starts talking about her funeral. It keeps her busy, it comforts her. She's especially concerned with the details of the ceremony, ways to make it beautiful and dignified. She wants to tread lightly, avoid creating problems for the family. She wants to leave a happy memory, a good impression. She's convinced that death is logical, or more exactly, she hopes it is: 'I don't have much time left to live. That's how it is, death is a right. But I don't want death to make a mistake and take one of my children. That's a disaster I wouldn't be able to bear. May God call me to Him in your lifetime, not the other way around … Well, that's what I wish for, I pray for it all the time, but who knows what God intends? No one dares guess, well I certainly don't. My father taught me never to think of God outside of prayer. I've always prayed. Today the problem is I haven't washed. I can't pray as much as I used to. I do my ablutions with the polished stone – you know, the black stone. But where is it? I've lost that too. Help me look, look under the sheets; sometimes it slips under the covers and falls down on the other side of the bed. You know, you can use that holy stone instead of water, you just rub it on your arms and your hands, it's just like washing. Did you find it? Keltum must have put it away, go and find out where. Your sister's gone back home, she's bored here. She says our TV doesn't show any good programmes, but the truth is she went because she doesn't get along with Keltum. They're always arguing and I'm in the middle of it. I watch but I don't say anything, because my daughter will be angry with me if I side with Keltum and Keltum will leave me if I agree with my daughter. You can't imagine how awful it is. So have you found the black stone? You see I can remember, I haven't lost my memory, but the old memories come back as you get older. Yesterday, for instance, I saw my mother. She's looking very good, she told me she doesn't take pills any more because the Prophet made her better. She is lucky. Now you, you're my half-brother, you died in the summer at your daughter's, when you went to spend the holiday at her house on the beach. Don't worry, you're alive, I'm talking to you and you're looking away … I know you're going to tell me you're my son, my last little one, and I'm getting you mixed up with someone else. But it doesn't matter, the main thing is to pass the time! It's raining. I don't like the rain and I don't like the wind. I don't like the cold. I don't know what to do. I talk too much, that's what it is, husband. I'm a chatterbox. I'm going to be quiet. I'll take myself off to pray, and then I'll bless you, you and your brothers.'

21

I try to imagine my mother dead. I force myself to anticipate what's likely to happen. I picture her empty bed, her room in disarray or completely bare of furniture. I see her prayer beads on the floor, two or three packets of pills tossed in a corner and emptiness invading my life, keeping me awake at night, giving me vague aches and pains. I look at my face in the mirror and realise that I'm old, I've suddenly grown old. I have new wrinkles, my eyes are sad, there's no light, no presence. My mother is no longer where she was, last time. She's gone. The words of her doctor, my old friend Fattah, are ringing in my ears: 'You must come home as fast as you can, I don't know how many hours God will grant her, but be quick. You know I wouldn't drag you over here for nothing. I'm not being dramatic, she's very bad. Her heart, yes, that's right, her heart rate plummeted again. So see you soon.' Or – the worst – a message on one of the answering machines: 'God has taken what is His!' A euphemism that's perfectly clear. In Arabic, people don't say 'dead', don't write 'deceased' on index cards, but choose the words carefully, trying to dress up sad news in vague religious formulae like 'God has taken back what belongs to Him,' or 'She's gone to God,' the way you'd say she's gone to visit a relative. We also say 'by God's grace'. You have to wait some time before uttering the words: 'She is dead.'

I'm not superstitious. I write these words and Mother is dominating my thoughts. It's a Tuesday in December. My mother doesn't like Tuesdays. She's always avoided travelling or doing anything important on a Tuesday. I see her in her bedroom, the pale light, the television on. It's Ramadan, someone's reading the Qur'an. She summons Keltum just to sit with her. She complains because she thinks I've forgotten her. My last phone call was three days ago. I don't like phoning every day. I'm trying not to let her get used to a daily call, but she forgets and can't remember when I last spoke to her. She mixes up the days just as she sometimes thinks I'm someone else. That no longer upsets me. I understand her confusion, her turmoil, and I prefer not to say anything, not to point out that she's raving. One day my sister decided to test her memory, making her recall the names of all her grandchildren and great-grandchildren. It was unkind of her to subject my mother to an interrogation like that. I find it hard to remember names too. I don't forget faces, but I don't always retain the names of people I meet. I understand how you can get them muddled up and not remember each person's name. It's not necessarily a sign of madness or even senility.

I can picture Mother young and beautiful on the sunny terrace of our first house in Tangier, overlooking the sea. She gazes at the houses built into the cliffside. She comments that there are more and more of them and says: 'Poor things, they live in terrible conditions!' She's plumpish, her large bosom and short stature make her look bigger. She doesn't like the east wind that blows in from the Moroccan coast. In Fez there wasn't any wind! She's convinced the wind has always spared her native city. The east wind is Tangier's greatest fury, it sweeps away everything in its path, drives out the mosquitoes, blows away foul smells and wards off the evil eye. It makes people jittery and causes headaches. She's afraid of it because she expects to be faced with my father's bad temper. 'No, son, there was no wind in Fez, or dust, or people getting angry because of bad weather. Here in Tangier everything's different. You remember, my little brother used to say Tangier was the land of the Christians. He thought Morocco was no longer ours, but already belonged to the French. I felt like a foreigner – that's how it was, I didn't have any friends or relatives in Tangier. I missed Fez, I missed my family, I missed Moulay Idriss's mausoleum, and besides, Tangier was the city that took everything from me – my youth, my family – and gave me nothing back. I was only ever unhappy there: your father was miserable all the time, his brother wasn't kind to him. Anyway, they're all dead, God have mercy upon them. I put up with a lot, I held my tongue, my mother brought me up well. Oh, I must call her. Mother must be all alone in the country … what country? Remind me, I saw her last week, she looked radiant. I think she's in the cemetery in Fez, but she came to see me – for someone who doesn't like Tangier … Remind me, where is she? Can you see her? Speak to her, tell her I'm tired, and if the train leaves, I'll join her. There's no train? I know there's no train, or boat, but we must all go to meet the luminous face of our Prophet. I'll say my prayer again. I can't stop thinking about those first days in Tangier. I have to bring out the memories so I can be rid of them. You were small, I can't remember, we were living behind your father's shop – well, your uncle had found a shop to help your father out, but behind it was a house. It was dark – you must remember, because you often cried in the night, you had nightmares. That house wore me out. At the time, Tangier belonged to the Christians. I never could count in pesetas. The Rif women counted in rials, but I couldn't work out the price of things, and I couldn't understand why no one used Fez money.'

No, my mother isn't dead. I just need to call her and I'll hear her say: 'Son, light of my eyes, beat of my heart, the one who's always looked after me, you've never abandoned or forgotten me, you've always rescued me, what would I be without you? I don't think I'd still be here if you weren't with me, your hand outstretched, generous, ready to do anything to carry me to the mountain top, making sure I don't suffer and especially that I don't go without. You, my son, God will reward you as you deserve, I know your kindness is your fortune …'

22

I arrive in Tangier a few days before the end of Ramadan. It's December. There are floods in Andalusia and rain in Tangier. Fasting makes people tetchy, aggressive even, especially towards late afternoon.

Mother is refusing to eat and, worse, won't take her medicine. She says it's Ramadan; between sunrise and sunset, only the infidels dare eat. Keltum reminds her she's ill and God forgives the sick if they don't fast. Mother protests and pushes away her food. An excess of zeal or a new contrariness? Has she simply forgotten she's ill, just as she's forgotten that her parents, her brothers and her husband are all dead?

She greets my arrival without much enthusiasm. I'm a stranger, or one of her brothers she's fallen out with. She hasn't recognised me. I'm a little disappointed, but I don't complain, there's no point. I ask her who I am. 'You're Aziz, of course, you come to see me every other day, your wife's always ill, your children got married without telling you, you don't go to the shop any more, you spend all your time at home with your wife. You must get very bored ...'

Then she carries on tearfully: 'You know your aunt, my sister, my little sister, she died. She came to see me last week, she was so well, she was talking and laughing, making me laugh. She died in her sleep, you know. She had supper, just a light soup, said her prayers and then death came and carried her off. It's odd, she's still young. I can see her right there, facing me. She's looking straight at me, as if she's about to speak to me. It's not fair, but it's God's will ...'

I almost believed her. After all, it was plausible. She spoke with conviction. Keltum signals to me that she's delirious. I phone my aunt in Fez and ask her to call my mother, to reassure her, tell her she's still alive and well. My aunt bursts out laughing and promises to call straight away.

The house is shrouded in sadness. It used to be a beautiful home surrounded by a little garden. It wasn't traditional but had an old-fashioned charm, there was something soothing about it. My parents had just left a house that overlooked the sea, on the Marshan clifftop. My mother didn't like it because of the relentless east wind, and the neighbourhood. Here, they were shielded. My father said it was solid, and he was proud that he'd bought it from the Rabbi of Tangier.

It was at the end of a cul-de-sac, opposite a little house where an elderly French couple lived. My mother liked them because they were quiet and, most importantly, they didn't leave their rubbish by her door. She'd say hello to them in French, laughing, and occasionally took them a plate of cakes.

Over the years, cracks appeared in the walls, the paint peeled, the plumbing broke down, the timber doors and windows warped: the house wasn't being maintained. My father couldn't afford to carry out all the repairs. It upset my mother. The house symbolised the state of their health: everything slowly falling apart and nothing they could do about it. One day, running a high fever, my father even came to identify with the house: 'Me too, I'm finished, I've got cracks everywhere, my pipes are blocked, my head's leaking, my legs barely hold me up. I refuse to walk with a stick, my eyesight's getting worse and worse, which suits me fine – I don't see the things that bother me. It's all deserting me, I'm an abandoned house, an empty house without a roof, with no doors. I have nightmares. If I'd had money, I'd have repaired everything, restored everything, I'd have turned this house into a small palace. But I'm no king, just an old man crumbling under the weight of his responsibilities, crushed by ruthless time. I'm a house that's falling to bits … Nothing works, the phone's out of order, it's a relic from the time of the Spanish, the wires constantly need reconnecting, they're so old you can't buy any more from Madani, the general store that sells everything. That just shows how time has eroded the things in this house, which is dying with me …'

The sitting-room windows are open to rid the place of the smell of damp. But it's no use. Damp's been here for years, it oozes from the walls and makes the heavy sadness more pervasive. Keltum and the other cleaning woman are exasperated. Mother's increasingly difficult. I can see it in their haggard faces and irritated voices. They can't cope any more. One says to me: 'I need a holiday. Send me to Mecca, I'll forget this misery.' The other says nothing. She'd like to go too, but daren't – she's made a pact with my mother never to leave her.

My sister's gone to Mecca for the fifth time. My brother says she's found a good excuse not to look after her mother. I ask him not to be judgemental. He agrees. He tells me he sometimes imagines my mother in a nursing home, a facility for sick, elderly people. Then he changes his mind: 'No, I can't see her in a room surrounded by nurses: she'll think she's in a hospital and it'll sap her morale. No, it's not possible, we can't do it.' I cannot picture her anywhere other than in her own home either. I sit close to her. I hold her hand and stare at the weird shapes traced by the cracks in the wall. I like holding her hand, something I haven't done since childhood. She's lucid and calm. She squeezes my hand. She talks to me about my disabled son: 'What do the doctors say? Will he ever be able to talk? God keep him and give him the power of speech. We must be patient. They're good children, a gift from God. God's putting us to the test, He wants to know how we treat a child who isn't the same as the others. It's important, son: they are angels, they're incapable of doing anything bad. In Fez we visit them as if they were saints, we want them to give us some of their goodness. He's a gift from God, we must protect him, follow him everywhere, never leave him alone. But what do the doctors in France say? Is there any hope? Has he been circumcised? Oh, all right, I don't remember, it happened here in this house, I forgot … Did you have a party? Circumcision's important. We're Muslims, aren't we? The child loves me very much, he kisses me so gently, he holds my hand, he knows I'm ill. He tells me things I don't understand. You should take him to Moulay Idriss in Fez. You can say I sent you. Our saint, the patron of Fez. You'll say prayers and our saint Moulay Idriss will give him his blessing! Our neighbours have a boy like him. They leave him out in the street on his own. Sometimes he opens our door and sits down with us to eat. He eats, and when he's had enough he gets up and goes. But our boy doesn't do that. He doesn't go into the homes of people he doesn't know. You must look after our angel! How many children do you have? I know you've already told me, but my memory's playing tricks on me. So you have children. And your wife, where is she? Why doesn't she come more often? Oh, there she is, next to you, I didn't see her. Tell her my eyesight's getting worse and worse. Come here, give her this bracelet; she can keep it till the day your daughter gets married. My mother gave it to me yesterday, she came to see me. She was so pale. She didn't speak, she just came up to me, slipped this bracelet into my hands and was gone. She's playing tricks on me, I'm going to tell my father when he gets back from Mecca.'

With Ramadan over, things are almost back to normal. There's less tension in the house. Keltum's relieved because I've extended my stay. My mother can't remember how many days I've been here. She asks to see the children – not mine, hers, the ones I don't know, the ones she's made up. She tells me about the older ones who come and eat and then leave without saying a word to her. She wonders what's happened to the very little ones, the ones she had when she was very young. I reassure her, they're at school.

'The M'sid, no? They're at the mosque and they're learning the Qur'an.'

'That's right, Yemma, they're at the Qur'anic school. We're all in the Bouajarra M'sid, in Fez just after the war, you know, the days when we had food coupons.'

It was freezing cold in Fez that year and there was no heating in the M'sid. We were so cold our teeth chattered and we couldn't remember the verses of the Qur'an, so the elderly teacher asked us to recite the Yasin surah all together. He told us that reciting it in unison would warm our hearts and our bodies. We all huddled up close. Some of the children were smelly, others pinched the bottoms of the ones in front. Some tried to stick their finger in their bums, it was a game, a humiliating ritual. When we came out of school, the other kids pointed at the poor boy who'd let himself be abused, called him a girl – the ultimate insult – and the stronger kids formed gangs and had the right to touch the weaker ones. I was spared, being too puny and too ill. The strong kids told me I was a sage and I should play the part of judge. One day I got hit over the head with a stick, I even bled. The teacher was furious and beat us randomly. That evening, my father picked up a kitchen knife and went after him, he wanted to kill him. The other parents went with him. The teacher came out of his house, hands behind his back, head bowed – signs of submission. He apologised and my father was relieved because he couldn't imagine actually using his knife.

The M'sid was a strange place where we learned the Qur'an by heart even though we couldn't read or write. Our parents entrusted us to the teacher and weren't worried, although my mother was appalled at the lack of hygiene and the lice she'd find in my hair. So she had my head shaved. That was torture. I'd cry and stamp my feet …

My mother can no longer stand. She fell over again. Nothing broken but she hurts all over. She's in pain and tells me her bones have become transparent: 'They don't hold me up any more. They're like paper, no I mean pastry, all crumbly. That's what my bones are like. You know I fall over a lot, my legs won't carry me. I have to drag them around like old friends who've let me down. They're tired of me, tired of carrying me, of never getting a rest. My eyes are giving up on me too. It's old news, but every day that goes by takes a bit of my sight. My eyes are slowly dying, the light doesn't stay in them, it's leaving as fast as it can. That's why I say the light in my eyes is you, my children. Come to think of it, it's been a long time since they came to see me. Unless I'm forgetting. That's it, yes, I forget. It's not easy, having no memory. And it's strange – old memories visit me from far away, as if from other countries. I don't recognise them. Maybe they're someone else's memories – they must have got the wrong house. For instance, I remember myself as a little girl, riding a horse, but it's not true, I've never ridden an animal. It's worrying, all these images passing by, getting muddled up. I can see you when you were a little boy, and my father hugging you, but when I get closer, it's not you in my father's arms, and my father has a funny face, too. It's strange. It's the pills that are making me mad. But I won't let them. So what would you like for lunch? I'm going to the kitchen to make your favourite food. But where have the servants gone? You see, son, I call them but they don't answer … Oh look, more visions coming through the house. I don't know what I'm saying any more, I can't see much, it's dark, we should turn on the lamps. Since we moved to this house, I haven't had enough sun: it's as if winter's living here, a long winter. I loved that season in Fez, when the cold bit my fingers and the tip of my nose. I'd wrap myself in lots of woollen blankets and I'd shiver and laugh. These days the blankets are thin and old, they're not wool but some material I don't recognise. When you hold my hand, you warm my heart. Tell me, am I staying in this house? You're not going to send me back to the other one, the one by the sea? I don't like that one. I know you won't let me die in a hospital bed. I'm so happy knowing you're here! It's been such a long time since you were last here, hasn't it? Twenty years? What, you've been here a month! Then I'm getting it all mixed up. Here, I must give you the coupons for the olive oil. I need it to make your favourite meal. Go and buy the things I need but be careful, Fez is overrun with foreigners who are making war. Are you talking about my brother? No, your brother, oh my son! Yes, he comes from time to time, he works a lot, they don't let him come, he has to ask for time off, you know, he works in … what does he do? Is he a doctor or a jeweller?'

'No, Yemma, he's an engineer …'

'Oh yes, he's in Khuribga, phosphates, that's it. He goes under the ground, he comes back up and tells the workers what to do. Ah! Khuribga! A city by the sea …'

'No, Yemma, you're getting it mixed up with Casablanca, my brother works in Casablanca.'

'Yes, you're right, Rabat is a beautiful city. Now where did your brother go? He arrives this afternoon. He told me that the house is old, it's falling apart, so he wants to sort it out, but where will I go? He thinks I'd be better off in an apartment. Never, never will I go and die in an apartment. How will they get my coffin out if I die in an apartment building? I'll slip through the hands of the people carrying it. No, here we're on the ground floor, I'll be able to get out without causing you any problems – like your father. You know, the ambulance came right up to the door, and he left.'

My mother has fallen asleep. She snores, her mouth open. She's far away. I hold her hand. She wakes up and goes on:

'You're not thinking of selling the house by any chance? Those people who came yesterday were viewing it, weren't they?'

'No, Yemma, that was your doctor and his nurse.'

'But I'm not dead yet, that's crazy, some people seem to be in a hurry to see me go. It's God who decides. There's no question of selling the house. My children won't do that to me, no. I refuse to leave. Only God can make me move from this room. I've got the funeral all planned. If we move, I won't have time to do it all again. Promise me you won't sell this old house! It's Keltum coming and telling me horrible things, to hurt me. She claims she's heard my own children talking about selling the house. She's lying, isn't she? She'll say anything. She's going too far, I'm sure she's got her eye on the house. The other day she told me about what she calls "penshun", the money given to people who are too old to work. We must give her something, she does deserve it, even though she annoys me and sometimes treats me badly. But that's only human, she puts up with me all the time, night and day, she deserves a medal. Promise me you'll think about it.

'No, I won't go to his house. I mean your brother's, he wants me to go to his house to have a rest. No, I won't leave my house, I like being at home. I know where the bathroom is, and the kitchen and the sitting room. I'm afraid I'll get lost, I'm afraid I'll lose everything. So I'm digging my heels in, like a donkey refusing to budge. You know in Fez, in the medina, a donkey sometimes stops and then no one can get past. He'll often do it in a narrow alley. Even if his owner hits him or gives him hay, he won't move. He stands there, rooted to the spot, his head tells him not to move. Well, so I'm your donkey, I won't move from this house, you can tell your brother that. And I'll tell my father too, so he knows nothing will change my mind.

'Are you bored? Oh, I know I'm no fun. Your father was witty, he used to make us laugh, but not me, I'm not talented that way. The other day a woman came and got angry with Keltum and Rhimou. She told them off. They cried. I don't know that woman. They say she's your brother's wife, but I didn't see her. They're inventing things, to stir up trouble. But you shouldn't tell them off, because if they leave me, who'll look after me? I need those women, I do everything I can to manage them so they won't leave me all alone in this big house where I can't move any more. So, son, what else can I tell you? May God help and protect you, may God place your brother's daughters in the way of boys from very good families, rich and especially from good families. Look, your father's angry, the plumber hasn't repaired the flush or the leaking tap. He took the money and didn't repair a thing. Your father's furious. Luckily an electrician came and mended the tap and the flush. I must warn your father that from now on, when we have plumbing problems, he must call an electrician. It's important, people change jobs so easily. The world's upside down. It's been turning upside down for a long time, didn't you know? Look, time has stopped on the clock face, do you know why? It's just because the wall's full of water, it's damp. Your father's late, he usually comes home for lunch at one o'clock. Oh, it's summer, business must have picked up. That's why he's late. Unless you don't mind taking his lunch to him? I'll get the basket ready. You cross Place Rcif, then Moulay Idriss and you come to the Diwane. And watch out for demonstrators, the king's been exiled and the whole of Fez is in uproar ... What are the protesters saying? Can you hear them? I think they're shouting: Morocco's ours and no one else's! That's what it is: *Al Maghribu lana wa la li ghayrina*! That's it, they want independence. My brother's with the protesters, he's an Istiqlali, yes he's Watani, he's a good Watani, a friend of Si Allal El Fassi's. We'll have to make them a good meal, because Si Allal's coming to lunch. Mother's in the kitchen, it's too much for her, I'm going to help. Can you hear the protesters shouting? They're hitting them, they're hunting them down. The Fez streets are narrow. What a day of madness! Here, son, take my hand, we'll go out and give the demonstrators something to drink. We can stay on the doorstep, the thirsty ones just need a drop of water. Fez is trembling because the Frenchies are wicked. They took our king and they're trying to take our children! It's good here in Fez. The weather's good, I feel good. In fact, Fez is the only city that keeps illness at bay ...'

'But Yemma, we're not in Fez, this isn't the summer of 1953! We're in Tangier and it's the year 2000!'

'What? Time passes so quickly! How many years have we been in Tangier, son? Count them up. Almost fifty years! But where was I all that time? It feels like yesterday. I can still smell the roses we spread out on the terrace to dry, to extract the refreshing perfume, drop by drop. The air's heavy with those scents, the summer's come to visit but I feel cold. How can I be in Fez and Tangier at the same time, in winter and summer at the same time? It's strange. You being here is worrying me. My foot hurts. I can't walk, I can't run any more. I can't run, but I'm still a young girl. I must go up to the terrace and hang out the washing and talk to Lalla Khadija, but my foot hurts. If I put my weight on it, I crumple like a rag. Before, I would have said a caftan, but today I'm like a shred of cloth, I fall over and have trouble getting up again. It's humiliating, finding yourself on the ground, waiting for one of the two women to come and rescue me. You see, son, I've always been afraid of getting to this stage – a leaking sack of sand, a bundle in the corner that can't move. I count the hours and days but luckily I get it wrong and don't know where I've got up to. You can mock me, well at least you're laughing, at least I can make you laugh. You know the washhouse roof might fall in. The house is tired. It's old, and the walls have drunk a lot of water. See, there are cracks everywhere. One day there'll be no more roof, no more walls, no more house. It will be my tomb. You won't need to take me to the cemetery; my

139

house will be my last resting place. No, for that I'd have to be a saint. Only saints have the right to be buried in their houses. I'm no saint, I'm just a woman who's tired.'

23

Is it because the telephone lines are so old or because of the damp that the phone's often out of order? Sometimes my mother doesn't replace the receiver properly after a call. The other day, it was Keltum who took the phone off the hook. Out of spite, a little act of revenge, a reminder of her power. 'Your mother's isolated, unreachable, it's all very well you calling, you'll keep on getting the engaged tone. You'll think it's out of order and then you won't be able to say horrible things to me. I'm unplugging it and the whole lot of you can go to hell. Next time you'll mind how you talk to me and you'll give me money for the shopping. I won't allow the shopping to be done by anyone else. I'm the one in charge of everything and besides, there has to be some compensation ...'

It's unacceptable. My brother went over and castigated her for her behaviour. She took umbrage and unplugged the phone again. She says she's a prisoner of the situation. Mother won't give her a moment's peace and refuses to let her go and see her many children and grandchildren. My brother won't give in to Keltum's blackmail, even if he acknowledges she's doing a job that neither his wife nor our sister is prepared to do. I can't see any of my sisters-in-law sacrificing their time and comfort to carry my mother to the toilet, wash her, dry her and carry her back again in their arms, like a child.

Keltum's become indispensable. She gives my mother her medication on time, feeds her, keeps her company, makes conversation, changes her clothes, even makes her laugh. Why would she do all that? It's paid work, but there's also a bond, a kind of friendship, a close companionship that's lasted almost twenty years. Of course Keltum profits from the situation a bit, steals from time to time, sells off utensils and antique dishes, and siphons off some of the housekeeping money which she's managed to persuade us to give her directly. Why would she be with my mother solely for sentimental reasons? My mother mixes everything up – job, affection, duty, etc. It's not a factory. As they say: 'We're fond of each other. This is the way God willed it, fate has brought us together and only death will part us. We've made our pact, that's the way it is. We are believers and God is our witness. Besides, we don't know which of us will be the first to go!'

Tangier is bathed in brilliant sunshine. I offer to take my mother out for a drive. She hasn't been out since the time we went to the Mirage. That was last summer. Keltum carries her to the car and we go off to see the sea. She doesn't recognise the streets, she's happy and she blesses me. I wanted her to see the people going by, to breathe in the smells of the city, watch a boat coming into port. I stop the car by the beach: the strong sun dazzles her. I realise she can't see much, not only because of her eyesight but also because she's so tiny. She's hunched up in the seat and hasn't the strength to sit up. She laughs it off, saying she's slumped in the seat like a sack of potatoes. We leave the seafront and head towards the Vieille Montagne. There, deadly serious, she says to me: 'Are we at Moulay Idriss's mausoleum, or not yet?'

'But Yemma, Moulay Idriss is in Fez, and we're in Tangier. The patron saint of the city is Sidi Bouaraquia!'

'No, I want to visit Moulay Idriss, I've owed him this visit such a long time. He's the one interceding between me and our Prophet. I entrust him with my prayers, and he relays them to our holy Prophet. I want to tell him to watch over my son, who's sitting his exams. You know, the youngest one's going to college, but he has to pass his exams.'

'But Yemma, Fez is a long way away, it's a five-hour drive.'

'Oh, all right, we're not in Fez or Meknès. Then take me home. At least I know where I am there.'

When we got home, she found it hard to settle. That evening she was very tired, and she had a bad night. Keltum tells me the sea air is bad for her and gives her diarrhoea! She makes it clear that Mother's personal hygiene is becoming more and more difficult – she refuses to wear pads and she removes the adhesive strips so they're unusable. Keltum complains that there's no washing machine. She says she's had enough, she's doing it all out of loyalty.

24

Roland's mother has moved out of her apartment to a small hotel in a quiet street in Lausanne. She's happy to stay there while her landlord carries out some building works. She's developed a taste for hotel life. Everything's easy, she has no worries and all the time in the world to read, watch her favourite TV programmes or phone her bridge partner friend. She discussed it with Roland, who encouraged her to extend her stay. He'd have preferred a luxury establishment, with a pool and a sauna. He's always liked grand hotels, he's even planning to end his life in the finest suite of a big luxury hotel. He's not sure if it should be in Switzerland or Asia. The ultimate luxury.

Soon I'll go and visit his mother, whom he often describes in language that shocks me. At ninety-two, she's on good form: she's independent, she reads, plays the piano and comments on her son's life. Listening to me discussing a novel I'd written about one of Hassan II's prisons on a television programme, she said to Roland: 'What on earth did your friend do to end up in such a terrible prison for nearly twenty years, poor thing?' 'It's not him, Mother, it's someone else, he's just writing about it!'

I have a fantasy that our two mothers might meet. Since mine's unable to travel, she'd have Roland's mother to stay with her in Tangier. I imagine the preparations for such an event. Repainting the house, re-covering the mattresses, redoing the bathroom ... If Roland's mother needed to go to the toilet, I daren't think of her shock at finding the flush broken, despite its being repaired countless times, the bidet with neither tap working because Keltum broke them just to annoy Yemma, a chipped washbasin, a light bulb dangling from the ceiling because the wire, held in place with an old nail, has snapped – and the electrician who's supposed to repair it is none other than one of Keltum's many sons who has no clue how to do anything. Can you imagine what the bathroom of simple Moroccan folk would look like to Swiss eyes! No, I'd rather they meet on the patio of the El Minzah hotel. I'll bring my mother in a wheelchair and tell her that an elderly lady would like to meet her, a lady a little older than her and in much better shape. She'll say that we must invite her home, then she'll change her mind and point out that Keltum's cooking is heavy and not always good. I'll translate the conversation between the two worlds and report it back to Roland, who'll have a good laugh over it.

My mother will say to me: 'This lady's in much better health than I am. Are you sure of her age, because I don't know when I was born. You worked it out so many times and decided on an age that isn't right. But tell me, this lady's Christian, isn't she? She's not a Muslim, I mean she's not like us, so she's an infidel, she'll go to hell – isn't that what the Qur'an says? I know that's not very nice, what I just said, but we were always taught that Christians and unbelievers would go to hell, so your friend's mother won't go to paradise, I won't see her there!'

'But Yemma, you know very well that it's people's actions that determine whether their soul will end up in hell or in paradise. A Muslim can be punished for the bad things he's done and go to hell, and a Christian who's done good in his life will be rewarded and his soul accepted into paradise!'

'Oh yes, you're right! Your father was always making comments about non-Muslims behaving so much better than Muslims. He used to say: "That Jew deserves to be a Muslim, or that Christian is so good, he's almost one of us!"'

She'll ask me a dozen times who this lady is, why she's come, what her son's name is, what her husband does … She'll ask me these questions until the lady fades into the limbo of her childhood memories.

I spoke to my mother on the phone this morning. She knew who I was immediately. The results of her tests aren't good. Her blood sugar level has risen, despite the insulin and her diet. On top of that, she's had a urinary infection. It was her doctor who told me, she was too embarrassed to tell me about it. She simply asked when I'd be coming to see her. She mentioned Eid al-Adha, the festival when the sheep is sacrificed, which had taken place more than a month earlier. 'Son, Eid al-Adha has always been an ordeal as far as I'm concerned. I had to put up with your father's nerves – he'd always wait till the last minute to buy a sheep, thinking he'd get a bargain, but often he'd be cheated. And I had no help. All the servants went home to their own families for the holiday, of course, and I'd be left alone with a slaughtered sheep in the yard or the kitchen and I had to prepare meals and do the housework. And then you were never happy: the first day the meat's too fresh, it's not edible. Oh, I remember very well, son, and don't tell me I'm talking nonsense. Eid holidays are always disastrous. God forgive me but they wore me out, and of course people are only thinking about their bellies, when it's a holiday that's meant to be about the poor. Don't forget to buy a sheep, even if you don't like the meat. You have to sort that out. You only need to share it among the poor. Then, after the sheep, cakes had to be made, the family came over to celebrate with us and I didn't have any good clothes. I'd be annoyed, and curse the wind and these traditions … Why don't the Christians have such messy holidays? All that bloodshed, the guts and the slaughter, and that meat you have to eat, which they say isn't good for the heart. I don't want to sound like a bad Muslim, but one day someone will have to free us from these chores, this exhaustion. Every year, on the seventh day of the holiday, I get ill, I go to bed, I'm completely wiped out. I can't bear it any more. Next year we'll buy the meat at the butcher's and then there won't be any blood in my house ...'

She thinks it's next week and reminds me that I have to buy a sheep and distribute the meat to the poor. She adds that it's best to give Keltum the money to buy what she wants. I did all that at the time of the festival. I tell Mother not to worry. I want and need to go and spend a few days with her, I need to talk to her, to ask her why the upbringing she gave me didn't prepare me for the ways people trick you. She'll tell me that you have to carry on regardless. She's always kept a distance, looked after her home and her children, she's never voiced envy or jealousy of the people around her. I look at her and I see, or rather I imagine, all that she's endured in silence, never crying out, never protesting, never demanding justice. I've always detected in her attitude, her voice and her words something that marked her as the victim, the innocent unable to defend or avenge herself. Victim of whom, of what? I don't know. Perhaps she didn't experience the joys and pleasures she'd hoped for from life. In the early days of her widowhood, I noticed that her general condition had improved. She was relieved, as if my father's death had liberated her, given her some rest, almost a summer holiday. She had been waiting for that moment, saying: 'May God grant me even one day to live a full life, without that man!'

I can't tell her that 'marriage is a work in progress'. The words won't translate into colloquial Arabic. She'll look at me

149

as if to make sure that I'm not laughing at her and then say: 'What on earth do you know about life?' She'll tell me that here, 'Everyone should know their place. We let things take their course; the path was forged by our ancestors, so we get through life as best we can. Some do well, others spend their days moaning. Me, I turn to God and give thanks.' 'What kind of life have I had?' she asks me one day. She answers with a long sigh and then changes the subject. It's up to me to guess at that life.

25

Keltum tells my mother that she's tempted to go to the literacy classes at the mosque: 'The new king wants to teach us to read and write. It's too late, but if we can at least learn numbers, I'll be able to phone my children and grandchildren.' Rhimou wants to enrol for the evening classes too. My mother's panic-stricken. 'That's what it is, you're all trying to get rid of me, you're doing everything possible to make my blood pressure go up. You're acting like young girls off to the mosque, leaving me on my own to die quickly, without my children here. While you're about it, take my daughter Touria with you – and my mother, she'll be only too happy to abandon me. Forget what this new king says – did he think of me, did he have a thought for people who depend on others? No, he just wants ignorant people to stop being ignorant. That's fine by me, but why take Keltum and Rhimou from me? No, you're being crazy and spiteful. I would never have done that to one of you. And who's going to look after my little brother who's ill? I know you're going tell me he died ages ago, that I'm raving, that I've lost my mind. I know all that, but my little brother is not dead. He's here, he's right next to me. You can go, but he'll stay by my bedside. Even though he's ill, he won't abandon me. He's handsome and gentle, he's my favourite brother. I told his wife that the other day, when we were at my son's circumcision. She was so happy, she burst into tears. Go on then, go to the mosque, say your prayers and don't come back. Learn to read! But what use will that be? I for one never had that opportunity. You want to learn to read so you can follow the Christians' soap operas, the ones with the actors speaking an Arabic that none of us understands. That's what it is, it's just so you can go on watching TV. It's a joke, isn't it? You want to have a good laugh, you're just trying to pull my leg and upset me! I'll complain to my son, he's coming in a bit. No, not the one who lives in France, no, the one from Casa, what's his name?'

Keltum and Rhimou begin to laugh. Reassured, my mother tells them to go to the devil.

As soon as she sees me, she warns me: 'Keltum is not happy. I couldn't hold my water in, it escaped, so everything had to be changed: the clothes, the sheets, the blanket, and even the carpet.'

'Why the carpet?'

'I have no idea, that's just how it is. Apparently the carpet's dirty. But it wasn't me that made it dirty. It's hard to make them believe that, though. Maybe it's a good thing if they learn to read. But I don't want them to, I don't want to find myself alone with two women who'll think they're better than me because they can decipher letters! Because once they've learned the alphabet, they'll imagine they're teachers, doctors, wise women. I know them. Son, tell me, have you thought of giving them some money on top of their wages? It's good to be generous; if they see money, they'll forget about the mosque and evening classes. I know they annoy me, but they deserve more than money. If I could leave them this house – well, something – I'm whispering this, because if my father hears me, he'll tell me off and then your brother will be angry. But I'm not attached to the dirt of life. I'm going to God with empty pockets and my heart full of love for the Prophet, so I have no need of material things.'

26

Roland's mother is called Zilli, short for Cecilia. He had a scare the other day when the hospital called and told him she'd had a fall and didn't feel at all well. He asked to speak to her. Zilli didn't recognise her son. 'I don't know any Roland, monsieur. You are disturbing me. I don't have a son, so don't try and tell me I do. I've never had a child, so leave me in peace, monsieur!' This is the first time her memory's failed her. Roland was hurt, he couldn't believe what he'd just heard: What, me, Zilli's only son, relegated to the status of stranger? Unthinkable.

He called her a few days later. She recognised him instantly. He laughed and asked her why she'd mistaken him for a stranger the previous time.

'Roland darling, the older one gets, the more comical one becomes!'

I take the train to Lausanne. Roland's waiting for me at the Hôtel de la Paix.

Zilli's closest friend is a very wealthy woman. Unable to walk any more, she's been given a place in Switzerland's most luxurious old people's home. Because Zilli's still independent, she's only entitled to spend a fortnight there every six months. Her friend has a Rolls Royce and a chauffeur, and from time to time she picks Zilli up and takes her for a drive. She enjoys these outings.

My mother has no friends left. Her friends were her cousins, a few neighbours, and women she'd meet at the hammam. They'd talk, moan, help each other out, lend each other party dresses and jewellery, then would lose touch when one of them moved away. My mother would have liked to have real friends, women she could confide in. In Tangier, our neighbour was a cousin of the king's. My mother admired her understated elegance, but she was often away in Rabat. When she came back, she'd tell my mother all about her stay at the palace, and the gifts she'd received from the king. One day she gave my mother a handful of sandalwood, the fragrance of paradise. My mother was so happy, she decided to keep it for her funeral. With her cousins, there'd be outbursts of jealousy and petty squabbles. My mother hated conflict and she'd be the one to calm them down. She was seen as a peace-maker, full of wisdom. But she'd never had close, loyal friends. No one will come and take her out for a drive in a Rolls. No one will come and chat to her. She knows this and often mentions it. 'That's how it is. The only friend I have is in Casablanca. She's my closest cousin and also my sister-in-law. She had that disease – I don't want to say its name. They took away her breast and she's been fine ever since. It's been a long time since we saw each other. That's only to be expected – she lives in Casablanca and Tangier isn't exactly near. When I was young, her husband – my little brother, the one who died at forty – would often come to visit. He'd take me out in his car and show me the city and the surrounding countryside. I loved him very much. The day he died, I thought I'd follow him to the grave. Our hearts were scalded; we couldn't get over it. He came to see me the other day. He hasn't changed, he was still well-dressed and he smelled good. He told me his older brother lent him some more money and that he isn't working. I consoled him. I told him it wasn't his fault, it's his wife's. She keeps him in their bed instead of letting him go out to work. I must call my cousin to let her know the latest about her husband. He's really doing well. Do you remember, son, those summers in Casablanca? I'd leave you and your brother there for the entire holiday. Oh look, while I'm talking to you, I can see him. He's appeared like an angel, a sudden light. I can hear him murmuring soothing things. Come, sit down, little brother. You see what's become of me? A thing, a clod of earth, a sack of sand leaking out everywhere. How many years is it since you left us? Thirty-five? As many as that? No, you're exaggerating, I remember it as if it were yesterday. You went into hospital for a liver test and came out all pale and cold. You died that same night.

My mother fainted and your seven children didn't know what to do with their colossal grief.

'Why are you crying, son? It's not you I'm talking to, I'm with my little brother. Go and fetch some fruit, the trees are weighed down with it.'

We're in Imouzzer, staying with my aunt, my mother's younger sister, the one who married a handsome, rich, sophisticated man. He was softly spoken and never came to see us empty-handed. He was the first person in the family to have a motor car. I remember it was black. I walked round and round it, running my hand over the doors. I pretended I could drive: I got in and put my hands on the steering wheel, but my feet didn't reach the pedals. Imouzzer was a summer resort. It was cool up in the mountains and all the prominent Fez families had to have a second home in this little town. This was where I played at getting married with one of my girl cousins. We'd cover ourselves with a sheet and I had to show her my penis and she let me touch between her legs. There was nothing innocent about our games, because one day she grabbed my finger and put it in her vagina. I caressed her and she nearly fainted. Those are memories that stay with you. My mother wasn't fooled, and neither was my aunt, who said in a teasing voice: 'Be careful, if you want her to be your wife, you'll have to be a doctor or an engineer, because my daughter's beautiful and will marry the handsomest, wealthiest man in Fez!'

The house is on a farm. I like playing in the vegetable garden. My uncle, my mother's younger brother, is there. He plays cards with other people in the family. Between exclamations, I hear them talking about 'the attack on Palestine by three countries'. I ask my uncle where Palestine is. He shows me a newspaper: 'It's there, you see, right next to Egypt. It's tiny. They won't leave even that tiny strip of land to the Muslims!'

Zilli's expecting me. Roland's told her I'm coming to visit. She had the cleaner come and insisted her son warn me that her apartment's small and very modest. Like my mother, she's anxious to 'make a good impression'. She is well-dressed and stick thin, with piercing eyes, and speaks with a German accent. I give her a bunch of roses. She smiles and kisses me, then says: 'You're famous, very famous, you're often on television. Actually, you look better in real life. My son's not on the TV any more, and he doesn't come to see me very often.' Roland protests. Zilli interrupts him: 'Nonsense, you call me, but you're not here!'

I compliment her on how well she's doing: ninety-two and still sharp as a knife! 'Yes, but my eyesight's going, it's getting worse and worse. I like walking, I like dreaming, and reading too. At the moment, I'm reading Thomas Bernhard. He's excellent – powerful and highly critical. I love him and everything he says about Austria, my country. You say I'm in good shape, but I'm just a shack, an old, tumbledown shack. I often think about death – I'm not afraid of it. Anyway I should have died at the same time as Papa, my last husband: he passed away twenty years ago. Where were you, Roland? I think you were away on a trip. I phoned you and I got that machine that asked me to leave a message. Imagine telling a machine that Papa's dead – that's no good. Well, you know, I was pregnant with you when I married Papa, but he accepted you. I mean he adopted you. I've never told you that, are you surprised? What does it matter, you're my son and your father loved you. He never said so, but in Switzerland we don't say these things to our children!

'I'm not afraid of death! But I am afraid of hell – I'm afraid of everything that awaits us after we've breathed our last. Heaven? *I* certainly won't go to heaven. Maybe your mother will, but I've travelled a lot, rarely been to church, and I must have committed a few sins. Where does this fear of hell come from? From the Catholic boarding school where I spent my adolescence, in Italy, with the nuns. *È vero, la paura del inferno.* It was during the First World War, my parents were afraid for me so they hid me with Italian nuns. *Non era un regalo, no, ma la vita era bella perché dopo la guerra ho conosciuto l'amore e la libertà.* I love speaking Italian, I love the language, the music of it … My son speaks German, it's not such fun. He doesn't come to see me, at least not often. I'll tell you what I think: he's lazy. He says he'll come, then he doesn't, but his old girlfriends come and visit me. They're all still in love with him, but he pretends he doesn't know. I've travelled a lot, I love hot countries, Egypt, ah Egypt! Kenya, Morocco! Here it's sad, it's winter all year round, people are reserved. I have a friend who went blind, I like walking with her. I tell her what I see. The good thing about her is that she's not talkative – we walk and I talk when I feel like talking. It's very convenient, sometimes we don't say anything, lost in our own worlds. Me, I think about my son, and she about her daughter. We walk for hours, we stop to have tea, then go back again. It's so enjoyable. The only problem is that when it rains, it ruins our plans. Then I think of Morocco – what a country! I discovered it just after the war, the French were there, but I preferred the Moroccan souks. What light, what joy! All that dust and the people are carefree. Yes, I'd love to leave this poky apartment and go to a home for the elderly, but they tell me there's no room. I have a few friends there, it's nice to have company, especially when your children aren't around. Tell me, have you found a room? Lausanne ought to have more hotels. Oh, I see, you're not staying, you're on the way to see your mother. She doesn't live in France, she's in Tangier? No, I don't know that city. You see, I'm in a very simple apartment, I know you thought Roland's mother lived in a big house. I've been here for fifty years, I rent. That room there was Roland's room. I still remember what he was like as a little boy, playing chess with his father, completely absorbed. He was a solitary child. The municipality sends me a meal every day. It's very kind. But tell me, have you found a hotel? If only you'd told me you were coming, I'd have found you a lovely room at the Hôtel de la Paix, wouldn't I, Roland? And does your mother have a bracelet like this? Look, all I have to do is press and a doctor comes straight away. And there's a button on the phone for emergencies, does your mother have one of those? No? So how does she manage? The people who look after her can't read or write? How is that possible? The worst things are my bad eyesight and the fear of hell ... but I walk without a stick. It's wonderful, I go for walks with a friend who's gone blind, I love walking with her because she doesn't say much, I don't like chatterboxes ... Oh, if it weren't for this hell business, I think I'd have gone already. I know there's that Swiss doctor who makes up a lethal cocktail. He puts the glass on the bedside table and it's up to the ill person to take it or not. That's good, he helps things along, but religion isn't so keen. There's an association, I think it's called Exit. It's funny: depart, go quietly, leave on tiptoe. My son wrote a whole book about that kind of death. I think I read it, I don't really remember. I'm not brave enough, I can still hear the words of the Italian nuns – hell, purgatory and all that ... It's very good of you to come, I feel proud receiving a visit from a famous man. Won't you have a drink? Roland, give your friend something to drink – no, not water, that's no good, even if it is sparkling – offer him a whisky or a brandy ... Monique's very nice, she's very beautiful, sophisticated, clever, with very dark eyes. She often comes to see me, she's become a friend, but she's still in love with Roland. Now, Tam – what a beautiful woman, a little aloof, with a faintly superior expression, but what class! And Linda – very bright, sensitive and beautiful, she's still in love with Roland! No, I don't get bored, I dream, I'm always dreaming. I dream of my travels, the journeys I've taken, the ones I haven't, I dream of the sun, I remember everything I've done. I fill my days with all these dreams, I relive them and that's enough for me. I sleep well at night, I have no trouble sleeping – not like Roland, who takes pills. I don't play the piano any more, I don't feel like it these days. What about your mother, does she play anything? No? What a pity, it's sad not to play a musical instrument. Me, I've spent my life travelling, discovering countries, swimming, playing the piano. What about your mother? What? She's spent her life in the kitchen? But that's not living, it's not even human! I prefer to eat light meals. Roland, buy me some black grapes, the ones that come from Italy, just one bunch. I like to see them lying on a plate, over there on the table, they're beautiful, especially when the sun's out … Are you leaving already? It's so kind of you to have come. Tell Roland to come and see me a little more often, maybe he'll listen to you, but I know he won't listen to anyone, he has very set ideas. It's only my eyesight that's going, everything's a bit blurred, but I'm well, yes. Perhaps I'll end up drinking doctor what's-his-name's glass of milk. The fatal glass of milk, Roland says lethal … you have to see the funny side, it depends whether they give me a room in that home I like. Then I'll stay a bit longer, otherwise I think I'll learn to be brave. My son agrees. The other day I had a momentary absence, it was just after my accident, and I didn't recognise his voice. He got angry but it was just a lapse, a tiny little lapse, other than that I'm well, I can't complain. Today the concierge invited me to lunch, that was kind of him. I don't know what he's cooking, the main thing is not to eat alone. I almost married an Egyptian – that was a very long time ago – a wealthy man, but he went blind, and I didn't have the courage to look after an invalid, even though I loved him very much. That was before I met Papa – I've already told you, Roland. I think he was in love with me, we got along well, we could have married but it didn't happen … You're a good son, you see your mother often, God bless you. You tell me she's not afraid of hell? What? Is it Islam? All the same, it's a terrifying religion! She's happy to be going to meet the Prophet? How lucky she is to have such certainties. She's someone who believes, that's good. Me and faith … I don't know …'

27

It's the month of October and I'm a long way from Tangier. I'd promised to call at the same time every day to find out how she was. There are times when the phone's constantly engaged because the receiver's been left off the hook. I get annoyed, I call the neighbours to ask them to alert Keltum. When she answers, she's even more obsequious than usual, acts all humble, almost apologising for having to give me bad news. I picture her, shoulders hunched, adopting the air of a poor woman carrying all the world's pain on her shoulders.

Mother nearly died of dehydration as a result of a severe bout of diarrhoea. Keltum and Rhimou were beside themselves, not knowing what to do first: wash her, call for help, phone the doctor or her children … They watched her getting worse, the colour draining from her face, her eyes rolling upwards. It was gone midnight. There was no one to dial the numbers, the neighbours were away and the young man from the shop – the only person nearby who could read and write – hadn't come back yet. They communicated their panic to my mother, who started crying and calling her children, confusing them with her brothers and her parents: 'The time has come, today's the day, the fatal, dreaded moment. I'm going to die without seeing my mother, without my sons, and worst of all, without Ali, my little brother. He went to buy some bread and hasn't come back. But call them, tell them their daughter's dying. Tell them I'm a good Muslim. I pray. I don't know why my mother's abandoned me. I've always been a good daughter, always obedient and loving. But life is strange. My son's hiding and doesn't come to see me any more. Yes, I know the one who lives abroad is here, not far away, but he doesn't hear me calling. Make him come; I need to talk to him one last time. I need him to take my hand, so I can feel the warmth of his hand in mine. He is your master, after all. Don't laugh but Moulay Ali, my little brother, is lazy. Where is he? He didn't get up this morning, he doesn't really like working. Look out: it's coming out, it's coming out underneath me. It smells bad. I'm spilling out my guts, my heart, my desires. Come on, clean it up, get some big towels and clean up all the bad stuff coming out of my stomach. I'm purifying myself. I can feel I'm going. My tongue's heavy, it's all furry, and it's hard to move, or speak. I can't talk any more, I'm talking to myself, and those two are still bustling about, but why aren't my children here? I know

165

they're hiding and I'm getting weaker. I'm falling and there's no hand to pull me back, no one's gaze to reassure me. I see people's faces spinning round, not stopping, not talking to me. The night is long. I don't like night-time. Everyone else is sleeping and I'm counting the stars. But where's my son, the light of my eyes? Make him come, come down from the mountain. I'm emptying myself and I haven't eaten a thing today. That's what death is, everything goes, everything turns to liquid … I'm looking for an elastic band to hold back the sleeves of my dress. Where did I put it? I'm going round and round. That elastic band's very handy. I don't like it when my sleeves flop down, it's annoying. Where's Keltum gone, what's she doing? Oh, she's in the bathroom, cleaning up my mess, that's good. And that other woman, what's she up to, why isn't she coming to take me to the bathroom? I smell bad, very bad, this is the first time this has happened to me. I have to wash, I have to get up, but I can't. I've always dreaded this moment, when I'm like a pile of heavy earth, unable to move. I'm nothing any more, a foul-smelling little thing, waiting for her children … Go on, get the living room ready, get the ovens going, people will be coming from all over. Go and buy a dozen chickens – they need to be soaked in brine overnight, to clean them. Buy some red meat too, and order the bread. It's late, but no one's answering. I'm talking to myself. There's no point calling the doctor, he won't do anything. I don't need him, he's useless – like me, I'm useless. I know because no one's rushing to see me or answer me. God is great, God is great, Sidna Muhammad

166

is His Prophet, the last of the prophets. God is mercy, God is compassion. But forgive me, God, I'm in no condition to utter Your name, I'm soiled. I must do my ablutions, but Keltum and Rhimou are busy somewhere else. They're coming, they're shouting at me – Keltum's the loudest, she's telling me off and says I should know better. I'm a little girl who's been bad, who's done it in her underwear. I must be punished. I don't like the way she's looking at me, or her tone of voice. But I'm always so afraid she'll go away and abandon me, leave me to fend for myself.'

I listen to my mother and gaze at a long crack in the ceiling. I squeeze her hand. I'm afraid that with her illness, her absence, I could become more and more vulnerable. She's always said her blessing was a shield. My believing it made her happy. Eventually I convinced myself I was protected and had nothing to fear, until the day the sky fell on my head.

She'd always warned me to be wary of people claiming to be my friends. I didn't listen to her and was trapped by a squat, deceitful little Satan. It was no time to complain or to call my mother as witness. The idea of being protected is irrational, but I clung to it, more out of weariness and despair than conviction.

How old is Keltum? It's hard to say. All we know is that she's had six children, they're all married and she has twenty-two grandchildren. She never mentions her husband. Perhaps he's dead or disabled, hidden away in a corner of the house. One of her daughters has eight boys, which fills Keltum with pride. Some of them come to see her. My mother isn't averse to unexpected visitors; they bring life to the house, relieve the silence and boredom. She confuses Keltum's grandchildren with her own children, gives them names, incorporates them into her earliest memories.

From time to time, Rhimou's family comes to spend the day at the house. Mother doesn't protest, though sometimes she finds them invasive. She says nothing. It passes the time – time, one of her worst enemies.

For the past few months, she's been sleeping during the day and lying awake all night. Keltum and Rhimou moan about it. They say life is upside-down – pros and cons, light and dark, black and white, silence and shouting. My mother shouts as loudly as a young woman. She summons everyone to come and sit at the table, to eat and laugh. Life, no longer a tunnel or a dead end, must return. It's daytime, a beautiful summer's day in Fez. The weather's hot, you plunge your hands into the fountain in the centre of the courtyard and splash yourself with cool water. Everyone's here. Maybe I, too, am part of this flow of memory.

I'm sitting in a shady corner playing with boxes of pills. I watch the women to-ing and fro-ing. It could be the eve of a holiday. Mother's happy, she sings as she prepares the meal. Peeling onions makes her eyes water. She cries and laughs at her tears. Her younger sister's arrived, wearing a gorgeous sky-blue silk dress. She jokes with the men and says rude words, then bursts out laughing. She's happy too. She hints that if she's late, it's because her husband kept her in bed. My mother hides her face. They forget I'm there. I listen, I take it all in, amazed at how freely they talk; when they're alone, they let themselves go. They name the penis and take great pleasure in repeating words for the man's organ, describing it in detail. My mother modestly covers her face with her sleeve, but laughs heartily. The women dance, mimic the sex act and sing. Suddenly my aunt spots me and shrieks: 'My God, He heard everything! He pretends to be asleep but he followed it all, the little devil!' My mother goes off into the kitchen and one of her cousins leans over me, saying: 'You know we're messing about, you're not to repeat what you've heard, all right? Come, give me your hand, stroke my breast. You like that, don't you, it's soft. You little devil, you like that!' I knead her huge, heavy breasts and close my eyes. I say nothing, I promise nothing. I laugh and cling to her. She sits down and opens her legs, presses me to her. I'm in danger of suffocation, but she rubs herself against me and I don't think she's wearing any underwear. I feel something prickly, maybe her sex, which she's shaved. She says strange things to me: 'My little man, you're too thin, but your friend's not at all thin, he's standing up. That's unbelievable, a sickly child like you with his thing in the air. Goodness me, I have to go, but if you like, I'll come back and play with you after lunch. Would you like that? But it'll be our secret.'

My father isn't here yet. Uncle Moulay Ali has arrived, with my sister's husband. They're talking politics, raging against colonialism, and take no notice of the women's delicious frivolity. I say to myself: 'They're wrong, it's so lovely to see a group of pretty women happy to be alive.' Nothing escapes me where I sit. I watch, note and remember. The women are carefree, turning their backs on their problems. That's the impression they give. They have their own world, they don't try to encroach on their men's. Everyone in their place. But was that harmony, balance and equality? It was a question of conforming to habit. We didn't talk about such things. So long as nothing changed, we carried on. Eternal recurrence, stages punctuating our lives and our times. After marriage, pregnancy, birth, the celebration of the seventh day of life, naming, the sheep slaughtered facing Mecca, breastfeeding, the first steps, and so on. When it's a boy, circumcision, another celebration. And then the seasons follow on, we recognise them by the arrival of certain fruits in the market.

I don't remember anyone ever being ill. Everyone was well. My parents mustn't die, that's for sure. The great fear, the dread, is a car accident. In Fez, cars cannot enter the medina. They stay outside. Only my uncle has a car. It's a black American model, with leather-covered seats. Its number plate is 238 MA 5. I ask my aunt's husband what the MA means. He tells me it's Morocco and the number 5 is for Fez, so there are 238 motor cars in our city. In Casablanca, there are many more.

28

My mother's yelling like a child. Her voice carries a long way. She calls Keltum and Rhimou, who don't reply. They're used to her shouting for no reason. Mother's angry with them for leaving her to talk to herself. 'They're trying to drive me mad, they think I'm crazy, that I've lost my mind. I'm in my right mind, my mother can tell you that. It's strange, my mother is younger and more alert than I am. I can see her rushing about, coming and going all dressed up, ready to go out, going to the wedding of her nephew – or her niece, I can't remember. I'll ask her later, she'll tell me, because if I depend on these two half-wits I won't be told a thing.'

The 1950s in Fez have the taste of small, very black cherries, the fragrance of orange blossom and the colour of a bygone era. Old age, then senility, have sent my mother back to the radiant days of her youth. People say she was one of the most beautiful girls in Fez. She blushes and casts down her eyes. Her mother's proud of her but says nothing, so as not to upset her younger daughter. What games did she play? Mother didn't play games but she learned to embroider. For days and nights on end she prepared her trousseau, embroidering the fabric used for covering mattresses and cushions. She sewed geometric designs that required great precision. If she made a mistake, she'd have to begin all over again. She even said that all the embroidering she'd done in Fez had damaged her eyesight. It was hundreds of hours of work. She also learned to cook, but that was natural; no Fassi girl could allow herself to neglect her culinary skills.

She loved setting the table and doing everything herself. On the days she cooked, she wouldn't eat. What made her happy was seeing the plates come back clean at the end of the meal – the fact that everyone had enjoyed her food took her appetite away, though she'd sometimes have a piece of bread with olives so as not to faint. At night, she'd be dropping with exhaustion and fall asleep before the others. She used to say that so long as she had the strength to embroider and cook, she'd be content. And her health was robust …

My mother misses being able to stand up, or walk unaided, so that she could wander through the old town of her childhood. This refuge in the damp folds of the past must be reassuring and helps her escape a situation she's dreaded all her life: being in the hands of others. She doesn't like those hands, or those faces. She needs to get back to the language, images, smells and voices of her childhood. Maybe she's thinking she'll come full circle.

We're all here, around her, but she doesn't see us. One of my brothers gets annoyed. What's the use? She's gone off journeying into the distant past and when she comes back, she'll let us know, calling us one by one and asking us not to lose sight of her mother, who's anxious to leave the house. We have to stop trying to find the logic in all this, and just be with her, even if she's not aware we're here.

Keltum would like the doctor to do something to help Mother sleep soundly. At night, everything's worse – anxiety, panic, the shouting. All the memories that inundate her and make her feel as if she's drowning. Her own daughter comes to see her less and less often. She doesn't even call. The two nurses who take it in turns to come and administer her injection and change her dressing are extraordinary. They're sisters who don't look at all alike. They treat her as if she were their grandmother, kissing her hand and speaking to her gently. They do a great deal more than simply their job as nurses. My mother's fond of them and is always getting them mixed up. That makes them laugh, and causes comical misunderstandings.

It came out of nowhere: a dark lid covered the sky, the house, even the bedroom. Gloom, nothing but gloom and the sounds of after-lunch life: the call to prayer, the clatter of crockery, the dialogue of a Brazilian soap opera in classical

Arabic, the saucepan vendor crying his wares, Keltum arguing loudly with Rhimou, the water babbling – or rather gurgling – in the ancient pipes in the bathroom, the neighbours shouting, as they do at the same time every day, the city's clamour, and my mother who can no longer see. She broke her old glasses and slipped off the mattress, and was about to lean on the basin to get to the table where the telephone sits. Why did she take the risk of falling again and breaking a bone? 'When I can't see any more, I need to talk to my mother. I know she's not here, but I call to her so she'll come and put her arms round me and comfort me, because this darkness that's suddenly fallen is frightening me. I can hear sounds of life, but I can't get a hold on anything. So only my mother can save me. No, she's not dead – not only is she alive, she's in her prime, as vivid and beautiful as a rose, bursting with youthful energy. I'm not making it up, I can see her, maybe you can't. I see her all the time. She's right in front of me, she's come to protect me, to hug me. We're going to recite the Qur'an together, she knows the Verse of the Throne by heart – the one that bestows blessings and peace. I can't see you any more, but here she is, she's luminous. I'm not crazy, I'm just tired from all these pills arguing in my body. They're confusing my mind and disturbing my train of thought. Now where are my glasses? Who's taken them? They're not worth much but they help me out. Everything's blurry and I'm used to seeing you. That's how it is, I don't complain. They're broken? Who broke them? Oh, it's only the arm, I can still hold them in front of my eyes to see. To

174

see you – my sons, my heart, my darlings. May God protect you and free you, raise you high above evil and above people who wish you harm – the envious, the hypocrites. Bad people, who never had their parents' blessing, the bullies. God shield you from their eyes, far from that black dust whipped up by the wind and blown onto the rubbish tip. Yes, children, I can see the evil eye is everywhere: jealousy, resentment and cruelty stalk the good, but God and my ancestors are with you. Don't forget to give me a beautiful funeral – don't you stint, don't be small-minded or mean. I want a magnificent send-off, with the whole family gathered around my coffin, and you, your presence will beautify and illuminate that sublime moment of departure. You'll give the day the light and the dignity it deserves. No tears, no wailing, but prayers, and me in the middle like a little thing to be returned to the One who made us, the One who gives us breath, life and also death. But death is nothing, it's just a stage on the way to something more beautiful than life, where the Prophet and all his saints await us … Why are you crying? What did I say that was sad? I'm just talking about our common lot – the end, death. Yes, be happy when you're organising my funeral. My body will be given to the earth and the worms, of course, but my soul will be with God, and I couldn't hope for a better fate … Oh, finally you're laughing. I'm making you laugh, that's a good sign. Me, I'm not afraid of death. I know it's all in God's hands, we need only obey and be faithful to divine will. That's what my ancestors taught me. I know things, even if I never went to school. In any case, I know what I need to know, which is that we have no choice. Where are my glasses, why is it so dark? Have you noticed, too, that the sky's gone completely black? It's already night-time, so turn on all the lights. I love bright light, it's reassuring and opens my heart wide. Never be stingy with light or prayers. I'm calling Keltum but she's not answering. That's how she is. She's been here a long time, maybe twenty years. I know her well, she knows me well. And still she upsets me, leaves me alone calling out to her, as if she were a precious, proud possession … Is that daylight? Is it night? It's sad I can't tell. What is this black veil over my eyes? Maybe it's the end, no, I can't feel the tug of the hereafter. I'm here and I'm waiting. Tell me why does Ahmed not come to the house any more? Does he know that another Ahmed, younger than he is, has opened a shop right opposite his and is doing better business than him? Oh, Mother, everyone says you're dead, come to me. My heart's overflowing with longing to see you, it's making it hard to breathe. They're all here – my grandmother too, the one who was married at twelve years old, Lalla Bouria, she's here. Do you remember her? She's your mother, she's been waiting for us such a long time. There's Moulay Ali too and your little last-born, your favourite. It's a holiday, but why aren't you coming? I didn't mean to break my glasses. It wasn't my fault, don't punish me. I'll be more careful next time. It was Keltum who told on me, she's taking her revenge because she has to be here to look after me. I dream about my last day all the time, but I haven't seen it dawn yet. How will I know? I'm afraid it'll come when I'm asleep. I say that because I want it to be solemn and happy. I say it so you won't be too sad, I want to bequeath you peace. I'm not leaving much in the way of possessions – I don't have very much, the house and my blessing is all. I noticed another crack in the bathroom, that'll need redoing. Don't wait till my last day to think about it. Don't let Ambar come, she hurt me when I was little. She's knocking at the door. I know her, she'll come laden with presents, but they're all poison. I'm not holding a grudge, but I don't want her here. Let her show her face elsewhere. I can see rats, too, in human form: there are three of them, three brothers who caused my father pain. You must chase them away. You'll know them because they laugh loudly, and all the time. But the day will come when they'll be suffocated by the harm they've done to others ... What am I talking about? I don't know what I'm saying, I'm talking nonsense, making things up to pass the time. What time is it? Have I said the sunset prayer? Or not yet? I can't remember. It doesn't matter, I'll say another prayer, you can never have too many ...'

Keltum rolls her eyes and says: 'This is what it's like all day long, she never stops. Sometimes it's her brother who comes but doesn't speak to her, sometimes it's her mother who visits and wants me to make a *pastilla* ... We're living with ghosts here, she must see them. I can't see a thing. Sometimes I wonder, maybe she really can see all those dead people holding out their hands to take her away with them. I admit I'm scared, but at the same time I'm still sane, I know she's hallucinating, but you can never tell. The dead and buried turning up in the house, it's spooky, but seeing as she thinks she's in her house in Fez, I feel better. It's all happening over there, and we're safely here in Tangier. She has no idea where she is any more. When her mind first started going, I'd correct her, remind her exactly what was what. She'd be shocked, she'd look at me in disbelief, and then say: "Either you're mad or it's me who's crazy!" She's been crying for three days, especially when the two of us are alone together. She sobs her heart out, not only because of her own situation, but because she claims her mother's just died and has only been half-buried, without her body being washed according to Muslim tradition. It's all very well me telling her that her mother's been in the ground for thirty years, there's nothing to be done. She insists it's so and goes on crying like an inconsolable child. Then she says her daughter's funeral was a bit run-of-the-mill. That annoyed me. I told her that Touria's still alive, that she's just come back from Mecca and that she'd talked to her on the phone the day before. Then she stopped and said: "If my daughter's not dead, then who did we bury yesterday?" "Nobody, you're imagining things, you're seeing things that aren't there."

Keltum comes into the bedroom, closes the door and sits on a chair, looks at us and says: 'Since you're all here, I have to tell you I can't do this any more. Your mother's my best friend, but I'm worn out, she wears me out. I need a holiday, a change of scene. I want to go and spend a few days with my children and my grandchildren, but I can't leave her. When I go out to do the shopping in the morning, she begs me to come back quickly. I don't want to hurt her. Twenty years ago, I cleaned for her. Now, I'm her friend, her daughter, her mother, her everything. And I love her too and I can't bear it when she's delirious, it hurts me. There's maybe fifteen or twenty years between us, but I'm afraid I'll end up like her, trapped between madness and insomnia. So I pray to God and I take care of myself. I too have my rheumatism, my headaches and my stomach aches. I try to look after myself, my children need me. Every so often I snatch a few hours and go to see them, sometimes they come and visit me here. It brings a little life into this old house. It's not easy, but what can I do? It's God's will that I should be with this good lady in her last days. It's the nights that scare me, I don't know how to dial telephone numbers and Ahmed rarely sleeps here. I panic when she's distressed and I'm afraid when I stand there helplessly and she has one of her turns. You should tell Ahmed to spend the night here in the house. He's a man at least, he could be useful in an emergency. Rhimou wouldn't mind. That's all I have to say. I've learned her medication by heart. Luckily, all the pill packets are different colours. Sometimes I pass the time going over her prescription: in the morning, one pink pill and half a white one; at lunchtime, two white ones from the green packet; in the evening, half a pill from the blue-and-yellow packet, plus a sachet. That's easy, I know she has to have the sachet before dinner. When the doctor changes her prescription, I panic, but I cope, I manage to work it out and I hope I never get it wrong. In any case, I've got good eyesight and my health is good. I'm at risk too, I'm no spring chicken and life is hard. Luckily we have this bond of friendship, I do good, you do good, and may God help and protect you.'

Not everyone shares this near idyllic view of their relationship. I close my eyes and let it go. Is there any choice? After all, it's my mother who wants Keltum with her and always asks for her. We mustn't upset this precarious equilibrium. As for Rhimou, who says nothing, what does she think? She does the cleaning, follows the Brazilian soap opera *Esmeralda* avidly, says her prayers and protests when Keltum bullies her. We sometimes catch a glimpse of the three of them behind closed doors: the sick woman, the woman in charge and the maid. There's also Ahmed, whose scheming remains a mystery.

29

I read in a newspaper that illiterate people are more likely to suffer from Alzheimer's than those whose intellectual activity has been more intense. My mother used her grey cells to imagine a different life, to shield us from harm and watch us grow up under the wing of her blessing. Her intellectual range is very limited: she knows a few verses of the Qur'an by heart, her usual prayers, entreaties to God and His prophet, and a few folk songs. So she lives with very few things coming and going inside her head. She knows the workings of the traditions of Fez by intuition and habit, how to find her way through the maze of the old medina.

Alzheimer's invaded this modest brain without resorting to violence. Mother sometimes has lucid moments and can laugh at her own failings. As time goes by, these moments are less and less frequent, and they're briefer. She's not in pain, she's bored, so she forgets the present and takes refuge in her distant past. She's alone, surrounded by ghosts and shadows from those kinder days.

I wonder whether Keltum's angry outbursts are caused by exhaustion and having to repeat the same words over and over again, or because she's afraid she'll end her life like my mother.

Thinking of this collapse, when the person you love goes missing and time stretches and disintegrates, you look at your own shattered image in that unreliable mirror and scrabble around for happy moments, hoping to fill these cracks in the soul and salvage words from this agonising confusion.

My grief surfaces. I must have a change of scene. I think of Zilli, Roland's mother, I see her in 1940s Vienna, beautiful and in love, beguiling, vivacious, travelling with lots of suitcases and trunks, so carefree, playing the piano just before taking the train to Paris, on the verge of a magical love affair.

Mother isn't mollified. She weeps and asks for her mother and her little brother. Keltum's at the end of her tether. She either snaps, declaring they're long dead and buried, or she plays the game and joins her in her fantasies. She put her in the wheelchair and pushed her all around the house, in pursuit of the dead. 'There, my love, don't worry, we're going to find your mother and your little brother, your favourite, too. Maybe they're hiding under the bed or behind the curtains. Hush, don't worry, darling, I'll pull back the curtains. Oh, they've gone, they're quicker on their feet than we are. Just a minute, let's go and look in the big wardrobe. I can hear muffled laughter, I expect it's them making fun of us. Don't move, don't cry, we'll find them, we've got plenty of time. Yes, I've made dinner, I cooked for them too. Your mother loves lamb tagine with quince and okra – she adores that slimy vegetable. I hate it. I know I'm a simple country woman, not refined enough to eat okra, but I've cooked it for your mother. Come on, let's take you into the sitting room. I can't see anyone, they're not in here. You say you can hear and see them, all right, but if you've seen them we can stop looking. That's right, we'll go back to your room. You invited them for dinner, that's good. I'll have to leave you to go out and buy some bread. You can't have a tagine without bread. I'm going to leave you for a few minutes. I'll settle you back in your room, then I'll lay the table and go to the bakery to get some warm bread. Why are you crying? You want a silk scarf, no, not a scarf, a headscarf, a dishcloth to play with, you want money to go to the jeweller's. Why don't you wait until your son comes and he'll give you some money, a wad of notes, but you take your pills now, while you're waiting. It's the yellow packet, no, I'm not sure, I'm worried I'll get it wrong. You're confusing me, I don't know what I'm doing any more. You're getting me flustered, I'm tired now. We have to call your daughter. After all, it's her duty. I know she's ill, it's the time of year when it all flares up. It's too bad. I'm here, I'll always be here, it's my life, my destiny, that God has written for me ...'

My mother's tired. The little tour around the house has distressed her. She says nothing. She's sad, her gaze vacant. She's gone, eyes wide open. She prays, again and again. As soon as she's done, she calls out to Lalla Bahia, one of her first cousins, and speaks to her directly: 'Lalla, ya Lalla, hurry up, it's a big day, the suitors will be here soon. The most important thing is to wear no make-up. Be modest and keep your eyes lowered, don't forget. Eyes lowered, I repeat. That's vital, it's paramount: you don't realise, a young woman who stares at guests is shameless, badly brought-up, from a disreputable family. Your honour's in your demeanour, in your silence. That's right, look at the floor throughout, don't look up except to thank your father and kiss his hand. Come on, Lalla, first we'll go to the hammam, then it's the henna ceremony.

'Lalla Bahia's about to be married. She's going to leave us and we'll weep for her. I wept so much over my marriage. How old was I? Fifteen, sixteen? I can't remember. I was still so young. That was the tradition, we didn't marry after the age of twenty. Can you imagine the parents' anguish? Becoming a thing that nobody wants, a *h'boura*, unsold goods at the back of the shop, oh the shame. I didn't have the time to get to the back of the shop myself. Now listen to me, Lalla Bahia, we're not the same age, you could be my daughter. Come and sit down, take my hand and listen to my prayers. I'm going to call Keltum, so she can get the henna ready, then the two of us will go to the hammam. I love going, though I can't really stand the heat. What luck! You won't be left in the shop for

184

girls that life has given up on – I mean marriage. I wed my first husband knowing nothing of life. He was a young man from a very good family, not rich but very pious and good. But God took him from me so quickly, He called him back to Him after a high fever. He was so handsome. I was pregnant. I had no time to grieve. My daughter was born and I began to nurse her. I had so much milk that I gave some to my little sister, too, she was barely six months older than my daughter. My father lamented, my mother prayed all day long. You see, Lalla Bahia, there's no need to despair. You'll marry and have lots of children, you have a generous belly, that's very important, and your heart is pure. You haven't met your future husband? That doesn't matter, you'll have all the time in the world to get to know him. What matters is not to lie with him before you are married. By all means lie with him, but on your wedding night. That's the way, or it will lose its mystery. You see, I hadn't met any of my three husbands beforehand. I didn't complain. They're all dead. At least I think they're all dead, because I don't see them any more, but where have they gone? Keltum, have you seen my husband? No, not the last one; no, the second one. No? I'm talking nonsense, that's what it is. See, she has no respect for me. Did you hear, Lalla Bahia? Keltum's talking to me as if I'm crazy. How rude. I've had enough, I'm going to dismiss her. Call my son. Tell him to dismiss Keltum. It's quite a big house, there are lots of people, I don't need Keltum any more. In fact, tell Lalla Batoul to send two servants. You know, Lalla Batoul, the matchmaker, the *negafa* with the three gold teeth. Why is Keltum laughing at me? What did I say that was so ridiculous? I'm muddling up the present and the distant past? So? Where's the harm in that? I'm not accountable to her. Talking of accounts, she'll have to tell me what's happened to the million dirhams that I hid under my pillow last night. When I woke up, there was only newspaper there. I'd counted the banknotes myself – there were lots, and all different sizes. It was my son in France who gave me that money so I won't lack for anything. Oh, I nearly forgot: tell the judge to summon my three husbands. They should be looking after me, it's their duty ...'

30

'It's hot, very hot. That's how it is in Fez, it starts getting hot from the beginning of summer. The winter's very cold and the summer's very hot. I'm sweating, pass me a little orange-blossom water, it's so refreshing. What do you mean there's none left? I bought the flowers myself, I dried them on the terrace and, with cousin Lalla Maria, I made about ten bottles from one litre. I'm dreaming, you say? That was thirty years ago? All right, fine, but is that any reason not to let me have the orange-blossom water? What kind of thinking is that? And if I want to eat *khli* – you know, dried meat – if I ask you to make me a little *khli* tagine, you're not going to refuse me that? The doctor says it's not good for my diet. But what diet? I haven't eaten anything sweet in thirty years, there's no sugar in *khli*. Oh, you mean the fat, but I have a good recipe with lemons that gets rid of all the fat. Where did Keltum go? And the other woman, what's her name? She pretends she hasn't heard me. People are strange. The moment you need them, they turn into ghosts. Oh well, we're in Fez, at home, Father's come in, his face is all lit up. He's always like that, his face is full of light. He looks happy, and tells us he's just bought a camel. We must prepare for the slaughter. We'll call for Larbi, the butcher, the one who married my last husband's first wife. You know, you remember my husband, who was Fattouma's husband, she couldn't give him a child. He was looking for a wife, to have children, that's why my uncle suggested he take me as a wife, even though I'd been widowed twice. He must have hesitated, because you never know, who is this woman, this bringer of doom? In the end, as luck would have it, he took me and kept poor Fattouma just in case. He repudiated her when I fell pregnant … Ah! I've already told that story? No, it wasn't me, it was someone else that made it up … so Larbi, who was to have thirteen children with Fattouma, slit the camel's throat right there in the middle of the yard. The beast shrieked like a human being. My father loved this ritual, it meant he could gather the whole family together. We knew that at the start of spring, Moulay Ahmed would go and buy a camel. Mother didn't even need to invite anyone – as soon as the camel entered the narrow alleys of the medina, relatives would turn up and move in with us for a few days. My father adored those days. In the evenings, he'd play cards with the men, and in the daytime he'd tell the local shopkeepers how he won at cards. He was a holy man, a wonderfully sensitive man, who knew the Qur'an by heart, but he didn't understand why women should inherit half a share and men a full one. He always spoke his mind. We were treated as equal to my brothers. What a remarkable man. I'm waiting for him, don't go. You know, he loves you very much. You'll see, he'll be here in a minute and he'll bring apples from Spain, as usual, and bananas, nuts, and dates from Arabia, as well as toys for you and your brother. He has a magnificent beard, all white, you'll see. We must tell Keltum to bring me the pot so I can start on lunch. I can't get up any more, but when he's here, he'll say a prayer and my health will be back to how it was before ...'

Keltum had someone dial my number for her this morning: 'I can't do this any more, your mother kept us awake all night again. Not only did I not get a wink of sleep, but I had to listen to her raving, answer her, pick her up when she fell out of bed because she wanted to go to the cemetery and wake the dead who are pretending to be asleep, the dead who spend all day with her, then abandon her at nightfall. No, that's it, I've had enough, I'll end up like her, loopy and deranged. But if I fall over in some corner of the house, there's no one to look after me. I've got my children and my grandchildren but they're all thinking of themselves, I could die for all they care. No, come quick and talk to her, or send her to a head doctor so he can give her pills to calm her down and, God willing, make her sleep. Do you know, she spent the whole night looking under the bed for Mokhtar. You're wondering who Mokhtar is? He's the baby she thinks she had last month. In fact, he's the nurse Halima's little one, or rather her sister's – she recently gave birth to a beautiful baby boy. She brought him to show us. She's so proud of her first child, you see, she couldn't know she was going to drive your mother crazy, because as soon as she saw him, she thought he was her own child. She wanted to feed him and started to sing a very old lullaby, then she refused to hand him back to his mother. We had to trick her into letting go of him. Halima cried and she hasn't come back. Your mother's obsessed with the baby, she calls him Mokhtar and she keeps asking for him. That's what's going on. She cries and says that the dead have gone, and taken the baby with them, that's why she wants to be carried to the cemetery, to look for Mokhtar. That's what I'm having to deal with. I come and go, in and out of this madness, and I don't get a moment's rest. I know she's attached to me, as I am to her, but sometimes, like last night, I run out of patience. The water heater needs repairing, there's a leak. The plumber says it needs changing, replacing with a new one, which costs money. And the pharmacist won't give us credit any more, he won't take cheques, he wants to be paid in cash. And I don't know how to go to the bank. Your cheques are sitting here, what am I to do? You need to come and sort out all these problems.'

My mother isn't surprised to see me. She thinks I live with her, that I'm my older brother. She looks even thinner. She says: 'Skin and bones, nothing but skin and bones. When I was young, I had the most beautiful bosom in the family. I

190

had curves, I was well covered, my bones didn't stick out. Feel my arm, you see, it's just old skin on bone. Keltum's making out I'm mad – do you know, she thinks I've had a baby and is going around telling people! The shame of it! I'm not mad. Having a baby, at my age! She's got the nurse's baby mixed up with the boy I had before you, who died a few days after he was born. We called him Mokhtar, then we buried him in Bab Ftouh – you know, the cemetery just outside town, it's a quarter of an hour from here. You go out, you take the first road on the right and it's Buajarra, then you cross Rcif, then you go through Fekharine … Wait, I think I'm getting lost, no, to get to Bab Ftouh it's simple. You go out, and as soon as you see a coffin carried by four big men, you follow it and it will lead you to the cemetery. That's where I wanted to go yesterday but Keltum's getting on my nerves, telling me we're not in Fez. I've never left Fez, why does this half-wit tell me different? She's the mad one. Isn't that right, son, we're in Fez? Your father's just opened his spice shop, he's in the Diwane, that's where his shop is. He sells cumin, ginger, pepper, paprika – wholesale, never retail. Go over there and tell him his lunch is ready, unless he'd rather eat there, if he's got a lot of customers. Go on, and tell Keltum we're in Fez. The Sultan's been exiled, and Morocco's weeping for its king, the men are demonstrating and demanding his return.'

'But Yemma, we're in Tangier, you're muddling up different times. Keltum's right, pray to God to give her patience.'

'How is that possible? King Mohammed V has come back and no one told me? What? He's dead? What did he die of? Why is everyone hiding things from me? It's making me angry. By the way, son, I had a bath yesterday with lukewarm water, it was almost cold. The boiler's not working. It's very difficult to find a plumber here, so Keltum heated up the water in pots and washed me as if I were a baby. It's true, I've got so small she thinks I'm a baby. Me, a baby! I'm still very young, though, I even breastfed the nurse's baby the other day. She left him with me, she gave him to me. He's so sweet. He looks like you, he's got your eyes, your nose, your hair … They took away my baby, you know. They said I wasn't right in the head, they gave him to a young woman – I think she was a nurse – to look after. I said all right, but they'll have to give him back when I'm better. After all, I am his mother. I dream of that child at night, you know. I'm with Moulay Idriss, in the mausoleum, with the baby in my arms. I'm having him blessed, I'm praying for him and for you all. As God is my witness, I'm always asking for His mercy and thanking Him for this magnificent gift, a beautiful baby with such white skin, which I love. You know, I don't like very dark skin. You'll be angry with me, but I prefer Fez children with white, rosy skin, especially skin that reminds me of my own when I was little. You may laugh, but it's true, I was beautiful – you can ask your father, he married me when I wasn't yet twenty, get him to tell you … He's dead? Oh yes, so he is, but when you go to his grave, speak to him, you have to talk to the dead because they're alive in our hearts. God says so, it's in the Qur'an. I hope you'll be telling me about everything when I'm in the ground, I like the idea of you talking to me, even when I can't hear you or answer you. You know, son, it's reassuring. I already said that to your older brother, the one who knows the Qur'an by heart, he promised he'd say a surah every time he comes to pray at my grave. The Qur'an softens the heart, clothes the soul in mercy and tenderness. I know because I'm this close to the earth I'll be buried in. I can feel it and it doesn't frighten me. The Qur'an, the word of Allah, will be with me. The angels make it so: for that, you have to be good and honest and have a heart that's pure, and I've spent my whole life making sure my heart's clean. I've never stolen, lied, betrayed anyone or done anyone any harm. When your father shouted at me and called me cruel, hurtful names, I'd answer him with a verse from the Qur'an. I'd say to him: "I leave you in Allah's hands, I'm just a poor creature faithful to God and his Prophet.'"

My mother points out that my friends no longer come to see her. 'You don't know how to keep friends, or you don't know how to choose them. I wish I knew what's going on. Before, Zaylachi used to come by sometimes, he'd bring me sandalwood and we'd talk things over, he'd kiss my head as if I were his own mother. He's a charming man, very well brought-up; he had a feeling for things. What's become of him? Why doesn't he come to the house any more? Even when he was in the government, he'd find time to spend a quarter of an hour with me. I see him on TV. He looks good, as if he's got younger. He's always standing next to the king. He's a good man. That childhood friend of yours doesn't visit either. His wife used to come and chat to me, and then she'd very sweetly go off. It's strange! People are fickle, but really, your friends are making themselves scarce. I expect I irritate them. I know I'm no fun, but after all they're your friends. I hope they haven't changed. My little brother, the one who came earlier, has lots of friends. I'll tell your father that Zaylachi's being distant. He must be very busy, he's a minister, a father, he does so many things. I don't do anything. Your father's in the shop and I'm in the kitchen. That's the way it's always been. Cooking, housework, cooking, eating, washing up, and your father grumbling that there's not enough salt in the tagine. Listen, talk to him when he comes, I've had enough of his temper, enough of his moods, he treats me like a servant. Yes, I know you're about to tell me your father died ten years ago! I know, but he comes back from time to time, he opens the door, tiptoes in, looks around him like a ticket inspector, and disappears. I can't see him, but I can feel him here, so I talk to him, I tell him everything that's bothering me. I don't leave anything out, I get it all off my chest. He listens and doesn't say anything. The dead don't talk, do they?'

My mother smells terrible. She smells of shit. She's soiled herself and doesn't realise. My mother, always so elegant, so beautiful, so particular … She's no longer herself, no longer remembers what she was. She'd have been horrified to find

194

herself in this state, but now she's oblivious. I look at Keltum, who nods to me. I leave the room while she and Rhimou take her to the bathroom.

My mother – who was elegance itself, always fastidiously clean. I remember the natural scent of her skin. My mother, in the spring, on the terrace of the house in Fez. She's just back from the hammam and she looks beautiful. She kisses my father's hand as usual, and he says: 'To your health!' We're eating on the terrace, which adjoins that of the neighbours. We all get together quite simply to share our food. Mother smells wonderful. Our neighbour compliments her. The sun is soft. I'm playing with one of the neighbour's daughters, while my brother corrects her composition. She has budding breasts. I am the doctor. She pretends to faint, I hold her in my arms. My mother watches from a distance, laughing. The little girl runs off to hide in her mother's skirts. I run too, my mother grabs me and hugs me tightly. She smells so good, she smells of a loving mother, a happy mother, a mother in good health.

Mother doesn't understand why Keltum's making her wash herself again. Keltum's in a bad mood, she's being very abrasive. My mother protests, so does Rhimou, who doesn't like Keltum's attitude. I look on from the corridor, entirely helpless. Mother's crying. She sobs like a child caught misbehaving. I look away. I say to myself: I might have come half an hour before or after this incident. Maybe Keltum left her sitting in her shit to make me realise how much she does when I'm not here. It's quite possible. 'This is what I have to put up with. It's all very well for you, you just drop in briefly, give your mother a kiss, ask her to pray for you and bless you, and then you leave. But I'm here all the time, coping with her sleeplessness, pandering to her fantasies, cleaning up her shit, putting on her pads, crawling around on all fours to clean the floor. That's right, your mother can't control herself any more, she pisses and she shits. Me, I've got used to it, but you, you pull a face and look away. I get the feeling I'm the one who's ill, I'm the one losing my mind, and when I wash her, it's as if I'm washing myself. And I think of her – not quite ten years ago she was ill, but she was still cooking, she was clean, she cared about her appearance. We'd talk about all kinds of things, serious and trivial, big and small. We'd even laugh.'

31

Mother is saying her prayers. Keltum asks her to stop making those gestures and rolling her eyes. She prays sitting down, in silence. But praying without first doing one's ablutions doesn't count. She claims she's clean, because she's just come back from the Makhfiya hammam in Fez. It's a hot day. There were a lot of women there but she was treated well. 'The hammam was full, Salma had kept me a place not far from the hot-water spout. I had three buckets, and she rubbed me all over my back, legs and arms. I had a good wash in spite of the women coming in from other neighbourhoods. Everyone likes this hammam best because it's big, clean and well-maintained. I must say, I can't wash in any other hammam and of course Salma's known me for such a long time. She knows what I need. She has the right touch. The other day, I gave her a gold bangle to thank her.

She couldn't believe her eyes. That's why I have no jewellery left – I've given it all away. I like giving things away.

'Where's my white caftan got to, the one I put on after bathing? I'm not imagining it, I remember perfectly well. I took it out of the wardrobe, sprinkled it with orange-blossom water, and took out my underwear too – white socks, my canary-yellow scarf, my embroidered handkerchief – everything I needed to go out. If you don't believe me, ask Habiba, she helped me get it all ready. What? You don't know Habiba? You're doing this on purpose, pretending not to believe me, you're all conniving against me. I have to say my prayers again, give me the polished stone. Too bad about the white caftan. I'll wear it after the next visit to the hammam.'

Mother isn't suffering, she's in her own world. The minute I arrive, she calls the servants to set the table and put the pots on to boil. Today she's decided we're going to eat lamb kebabs. She says she made them the day before and they're marinating with parsley, coriander, finely chopped onion, cumin, pepper, paprika, salt and a drop of olive oil. She asks Keltum to light the *kanoun* to grill the meat. She also announces that she's made a chicken tagine with olives and preserved lemons. She says she peeled two onions, then added oil, water, ginger, pepper, salt and a few strands of pure saffron, mixed all the ingredients, then heated them over a gentle flame. She reminds Keltum that the chicken absolutely must be a free-range, local hen, not battery-farmed. That's what she's cooked for us. Except that it's not lunchtime and there are no kebabs and no tagine. Yet Mother's overjoyed, inhaling deeply as if she's smelling the aroma of all these dishes.

'I'm not at all hungry,' she says. 'All these pills are ruining my appetite. But what gives me great pleasure is watching you eat what I've made for you. That's my joy. Whatever you do, don't tell me you're going to your friends' house or your brother's. No, I won't let you. Tell them your mother's spent the whole day making the food you love. So once the table's set and you're all sitting round, I'll eat just by watching you. Tomorrow I'll cook for your father. I'll make him his favourite dish – calves' feet with a little wheat and some chickpeas. I'll season it and let it simmer on the wood fire all night long. It'll be delicious. I've already asked Keltum to go to Bouchta, Fez's best butcher, to buy the calves' feet. They need to be cleaned and the fuzz scraped off, then left to soak in brine for a long time. You have to be careful with the garlic, you know, so it doesn't cause bad breath, you have to open it and take out the green shoot, that's the culprit. People don't know how to prepare it.'

'But Yemma, Father's no longer with us. He passed away eleven years ago.'

'Oh all right, he's dead. That doesn't matter, it's his favourite. We still need to make him happy – even the dead need our attention. So, tomorrow he can feast. What are you doing? Where are you going? The meal's ready, sit down … What, you're going home? This is your home. Your father'll be along any minute – go on, get on the phone and call him.

If he doesn't answer, it means he's on his way. He won't take taxis. He always says there's nothing better than walking, but I know he's saving money, too. Your father's never been a big spender. He's careful with his money, he hasn't got much, we live very simply. I tell him we'll be rich when I inherit from my father, he has land on the Imouzzer road, but he doesn't look after it. I know I'll have my share one day, but we don't talk about that in our family while my father's still alive. It's shameful to think about inheriting, and anyway you never know who'll go first. God has His secrets. I live in God's secret heart, He guards me and protects me from evil. When my time comes, I'll only have to close my eyes and profess my faith: there's no other God but God and Muhammad is His prophet. I'll say those words forever, until I am no more, until silence and serene night.'

I arrive unannounced. I find Keltum with two young women – pretty, expertly made-up, looking embarrassed, and both clutching mobile phones. Keltum says: 'These are my eldest son's daughters, they work in the free zone at the port, in the garment factories.' The girls get up, barely say goodbye to my mother, give me a sidelong glance as if we had dealings in common, then vanish. Keltum sees them out. I can tell she's uncomfortable. I say nothing. She repeats that they're her eldest granddaughters and they're good girls. I don't say a word, and she continues to make excuses for their presence. I understand and go and sit beside my mother, who says to me in a hushed voice: 'They're her daughter's daughters, or her son's daughters, she has so many children, maybe six or seven, I get muddled. The boys don't do anything, only the girls work. May God punish me for an evil thought, but I think … no, I'm not saying a word, I didn't even think it … Life is hard … They have phones they put in their pockets, and me with this telephone that's constantly out of order, with a cable that doesn't even stretch as far as my bed … Do something, buy me a phone like those girls have, I won't know how to work it, just get a receiver so I can speak to you. I've had enough of this one with a wire, when you call me – you see, it's tied to the other wire with a bit of string. It's not very practical. If I pull on it at all, I can't get a dialling tone. When it doesn't work, my heart beats like mad, I start thinking that that's the moment you're going to call and be answered by nothingness, so do something … Those two girls come to see Keltum a lot. I think they give her money, or maybe she gives them some of our savings. They say they have fiancés, but nothing specific … I've never had a fiancé myself, I went from childhood games to the nuptial bed, where a man was waiting for me. I was frightened. Facing the unknown. Just think, son, how things have changed. I would close my eyes. I've forgotten the rest. Girls go to work. How much do they make? I wonder. They have jewellery and shoes imported from Spain. Their father doesn't work any more. He used to have a lorry, but he had an accident, they found out he had no insurance and his licence was fake. He almost went to prison. They took away his lorry. Luckily, no one died, no one was hurt. So he's out of work. His daughters went out on

201

the street. Keltum says they work at the port but sometimes they come to see her in the morning, early, when they ought to be at the factory. I haven't lost my mind, I see everything, I notice everything, but I don't dare think nasty thoughts.

'Keltum's bored. Rhimou's bored. And I'm bored. Even the television spreads boredom. The coffee table's lopsided – boredom's got into the wood. The nurses leave as fast as they can, for fear of catching it. My sons are bored, I can see it in their faces and the way they move. I know I'm no fun, I get night and day mixed up, I'm lost in time, I lose track of everything, so Keltum or Rhimou's families come to chase away the boredom. Your father says they arrive just before mealtimes, to eat and then leave. Rhimou has two sisters, both of them fat. They come with their children, they set the table, they eat, burp and drink tea, making a horrible slurping noise. They're peasants, backward people, uneducated, but I accept it, I tell myself I'm doing good, helping people, and I can't stop them from coming. I'm giving alms, doing *zakat*. That's it, my father always told me we should give to the poor. I give – even if I have nothing, I give in other ways. When I see things I don't like, I turn a blind eye. I don't have any choice. No choice, son, no choice. My husband isn't back yet, I'm waiting for him and he's late, I hope nothing serious has happened. Your father's stubborn, he's always last to close up the shop, I'm waiting for him. Why not call him, tell him to hurry, the food's getting cold?'

'But Yemma ...'

'I know you're going to tell me your father's no longer of this world. You're wrong, I saw him this morning. He spoke to me, he even asked me to cook him calves' feet, so … Oh, I see, he must have gone over to Chama'ine to see Uncle Sidi Abdesslam, the one who arranged our marriage. They're friends – sometimes they meet, get to talking and forget it's lunchtime …'

'But Yemma, it's evening, it's night, it's two o'clock in the morning. Everyone's asleep. Keltum's asleep, so is Rhimou, and I'm dropping on my feet. I said I'd sit with you tonight to see if you sleep well, but your eyes are open and your mind's awake. We aren't in Fez and Sidi Abdesslam is long dead, and so is Father …'

'Well, they must be seeing each other in God's house. Perhaps they're in paradise, I hope so for their sake. So what time is it? I have to take my pills. What, it's not the right time? Why not? You must know what's good for me and what's not, son. All right then, good night, I think I'm feeling sleepy.'

It's the second time Mother's said to me: 'I haven't seen you since your funeral, I've missed you!' She's living in paradise. She really is in another world, because she's reunited with everyone in the family who's passed away. She spends time talking with them and has us believe they're here, among the living. But why did she include me in the procession of the dead? She doesn't want to live without me and carries me off with her, into her daydreams – her delusions, that in the end we find amusing. My brothers and I phone each other to exchange the latest anecdotes and we laugh, saying: 'At least she's not in pain.'

When I gently protest, saying: 'But I'm alive!' she laughs and adds: 'In any case, I wouldn't have survived your death. God will carry me off in your lifetime, I'm depending on it, so if I was talking about burial, I must have got you mixed up with my beloved little brother. You know, son, with this confusion everything gets muddled in my head – everything, people, time, what I see and what I feel, fruit and vegetables, medicine and sugar, day and night, stars and dreams, sleeping and forgetting, you see, son … Are you sure you're my son? Forgetting … I forget the main things but that's all right, I hope I'm not a burden to you and that I never will be. You know, when I lost my first husband at seventeen, someone said to me: "God has lifted the weight of life from you, a child already widowed. But life will not stop: your innocence was slapped by a sudden death, but see that you stay light all your life. That's important." And I wasn't sad any more, I felt as if I had wings. That's why the grief wasn't too overwhelming and I remarried quite quickly. My mother was lovely because of that lightness too. She was like a bee – lively, quick and graceful. I'd so love to be like her on the day of her death. She went in her sleep. I'll be carried off in my sleep too.'

The ghosts of the past must have taken leave of my mother. She had another episode this morning. Nothing's in its place any more, neither people nor things. I call out to her. She's crying, she's in distress. 'Come quick, please, come and bring me my children, the little girl I adopted has gone. She was with me in the bathroom, she went to open the front door and now she's gone. She's been kidnapped. She was too good for me, I know, but I'm worried sick, she hasn't come back. Where can she be? I hope she won't get hurt, so come, I'm on my knees, I'm begging you, don't leave me alone, there are people who want to hurt me, they're coming and going, I can see them, they're getting close.'

I find her very agitated, her headscarf askew. She holds out her arms and I hug her. My children shower her with kisses, she seems calmer but insists we stay with her. She can't see very well. Her glasses are broken. When we leave, she starts pleading with us. I'm choked up. The children ask why she's crying. We leave, promising to come back the next day. She understands it as next month and gets the seasons mixed up: 'It will be Ramadan, you'll come for the breaking of the fast.'

32

Zilli is dead. Roland's just told me. She was having lunch with a friend on the terrace of Le Mirabeau in Lausanne on a sunny July day. At the end of the meal, she started to cough. Her friend gave her a glass of water: she drank it and then she choked. She keeled over in her chair, fell head first onto the lawn. Roland was at the Pully swimming pool, playing ping-pong. He heard his name being called over the tannoy, it was the police. They told him the news. He went back to the ping-pong table and carried on with his game. He said: 'In any case, she was dead. I had to finish the match, especially since I was winning.' The next day, he opened the envelope in which Zilli had written her instructions: 'Please cremate me and scatter my ashes in the garden of remembrance. I don't want a religious ceremony or an obituary notice in the press.'

On the day of the cremation, there were a few elderly ladies, including her blind friend, the concierge from her apartment block, Monique and Naomi, Roland's current girlfriend.

My mother continues to deteriorate. Seeing her is less and less enjoyable. She's affectionate, but gets everyone's faces confused. She needs us to be there, which is why I go almost every day. Keltum's taken the day off. Everything around my mother has fallen apart. No matter how much Rhimou tries to reassure her, there's nothing to be done. One piece of the puzzle out of place, and panic breaks out. Keltum can't take any more. She needs a break once or twice a week. I understand. She reminds me she's not a domestic servant but a friend, a member of the family.

My visits get shorter and shorter. Not so long ago, I'd sit beside my mother and hold her hand, and we'd talk. But now, I'm loath to ask her questions about her health. It sets her off on a rant that we're forced to follow or pretend to understand. Funnily enough, she's most coherent on the telephone. Perhaps voices are more deeply imprinted on the memory than images. For the time being, I alternate: one day I phone, the next I come and see her.

Keltum has made a list of the household repairs needed:
– A new water heater, this one is beyond repair.
– Buy a new cooker.
– Repair the toilet flush.

– Throw out the old rug from Rabat. It stinks.

– Install a satellite dish so that Rhimou can watch *Esmeralda*, otherwise she'll go over to the neighbours' and your mother doesn't like it when she goes, even if it's only next door.

– Talk to the pharmacist and ask her to give me credit.

– And, if it's not too much to ask, buy me a mobile phone … Yes, I need one, so my many children and grandchildren can call me.

Mother is very busy. She barely notices I'm there. She's winding a handkerchief around her forefinger, then her thumb. She repeats the same movement dozens of times. She talks, talks to herself, is completely unaware, repeating words back to front. She sings softly to herself, hums, and then stops suddenly. 'Who's there? Oh, son, I didn't see you come in, have you been here long? My eyesight's getting worse and worse, son. It's dark all the time. I need light, light's important. Tell me, on your way home, you didn't see my father – you know, your grandfather? He was in town, I think he was having lunch with Moulay Ismail, you know, the one with eight daughters who's always trying to marry them off. Poor man! Eight daughters … Some of them have found a husband. It was arranged. He's a jeweller, he's rich. One of his daughters married a cobbler. Imagine – a poor craftsman who mends old *babouches*. What drudgery! He earns nothing. So his father-in-law offered to open a women's shoe shop for him. He was overjoyed. But because he worked only with women, he ended up marrying one and imposed her on his household. Moulay Ismail came to my father to complain – you know, your grandfather's a highly respected man, people come from all over the country to ask his advice. So I heard it all. Poor Ghita – her name's Ghita, I think – went to Moulay Idriss, to the mausoleum, and asked the great saint for sanctuary. She said she wouldn't leave the mausoleum until the second wife was repudiated. But we're in Fez and Islam always favours the man. Apparently the Qur'an says a man must be fair to all his wives. How to be fair? You ask what I'd have done? Well, I wouldn't have run away to Moulay Idriss. I'm not a bad woman. I wouldn't have gone and poked the second wife's eye out, no. I'm not capable of it. But tell me, who are you? And where have my three husbands gone?'

She's fallen silent. Her gaze is vacant. What is time doing? I'm not certain that it's passing. It bypasses her as if she no longer mattered. Time straddles this body reduced to so little. She is there, forgotten by time – rooted, stuck in the 1940s, faithful to her ghosts. She takes off her headscarf. Keltum snatches it from her and puts it back on her head, angrily. She tells her off. Mother doesn't answer, just lets her get on with it.

She asks for a mirror. Keltum hesitates. My mother insists. She looks at herself in a little handbag mirror that's cracked down the middle. She starts to laugh. 'Who are these two women leaning over me, watching me? They look alike. They're crazy – crazy old women. One of them looks like Lalla Bouria, my mother's mother, who died at a hundred, but what's she doing here? If she's dead, she shouldn't be here. Still I recognise her, it's definitely her. She was treated like a queen because after my mother, she only had boys, four boys, all of them handsome and intelligent. I don't know who the other one is. Maybe she's my mother, but my mother isn't dead, she just had lunch with us. But whose white, grey, lanky hair is that? She should have kept it under a canary-yellow scarf. I love that colour, it gladdens my heart. Here, take your broken mirror. You're the one that broke it. They've broken everything in this house. They'd break me too, if they could. But here's my son, watching over everything, and my father comes to see me twice a day too. Who's living in this mirror? Can you see what I see? It's strange, he looks like Moulay Ali, my brother. To think everyone told me he was dead when he's never left the house, he's just moved, come to find refuge here. His wife doesn't understand him, she's stirring up trouble. Look, take this mirror, it's big enough to hide my little brother! Can you hear, he's talking to me, he says he's waiting for our father to arrive so he can come out of hiding. People often say the mirror never lies. It's true. He's so handsome, my Moulay Ali! Oh, if only his wife could see him. She tells everyone he's dead, but my brother's alive, I have proof. Go and look in the other mirrors, the house is full of them, see if your father – who really is dead and buried – isn't trying to slip behind the big mirror in the passage, the one he bought from the Rabbi of Tangier. He said it was a mirror that came from afar, from a city on the water, in Europe. Oh, these looking glasses hold so many surprises for us! Now I hear my father's footsteps, I see he's holding a child's hand, but who is the child? Maybe it's Abdelkrim, the one who was carried off by a high fever. He's handsome, he was four years old when the angels came to take him. He left … like an angel. But why's my father bringing him back? The two of them are coming from paradise. Unless the mirrors … the mirrors are playing tricks on me. I'm not crazy, I can see my father and he's leaning over me, I'm trying to kiss his hand, he pulls it away. You, you can't see a thing – but open your eyes, son, it's your grandfather, Moulay Ahmed, the man all Fez adores and worships, he's never hurt anyone, he hasn't even had a bad thought about anyone … The mirror will tell you that. But who's taken my Monica? She's so pretty, my rag doll, sewn from the Jewish tailor's scraps. I drew her in my head and Moishe the Jew gave me the wool and some remnants. It's summer, Fez is hot, but Moishe isn't hot in his black djellaba. He works without looking up. My mother's brought him lunch: hardboiled eggs and tomatoes. He doesn't eat our food, he's sorry because he can smell the food cooking and he tells Mother he'd have liked to try it but his religion doesn't allow it. Yesterday he brought me a cracker made with white flour and no salt. I ate it out of curiosity, it had no taste. Moishe is a good mattress-maker. He's always worked for our family.

'Where's my Monica? My doll? That's odd, I was playing brides with her. It was my little sister who stole her. She's jealous, she thinks she's cleverer than me. Too bad. I won't say a word, I'm going to consult the mirror, at least it never lies. When I look at my reflection, I see another world, strange people moving around me. I don't know where I am any more. It's the pills again. Those pills are making me crazy, that's what Keltum told the doctor the other day. How do I tell her I'm not deranged, I'm on a journey, and sometimes I stop in the city of my childhood and I'm with my parents again, and all my things, my smells. You know, I can't stand the smell of that donkey, Keltum. She doesn't hear me, she's gone out, so I can tell you she's a donkey. That woman scares me. Where am I? My head's spinning, I want to sleep, don't leave me, stay here beside me. Give me your hand ...'

And so my mother has only memories. They take up all the space. When I see her, nothing happens. My mother has quietly left. She no longer talks of her funeral because she thinks she's already dead and buried. She's already on the other side. It distresses me and I say nothing.

33

Mother is no longer able to speak: she has difficulty forming her words. I can't understand what she's saying. I catch one word and guess the rest. Her face has a strange pallor, her eyes stare at the ceiling. The doctor has removed her dentures. Her mouth's a hole, her bottom lip swallowed up by the hole. Her hands are very thin. She's lying on her back, not moving. If anyone touches her, she lets out a whimper. She's absent or she snores. We have to keep an eye on her blood sugar, her temperature, her perspiration. We have to bathe her glassy eyes.

I sit close to her and take her hand. She asks for her children. We're all here, apart from Touria, who's gone to Mecca.

Her doctor, whom she never fails to recognise, visits her every morning and evening. At the moment, I'm talking to her, telling her about my childhood: 'You're much thinner.

Do you remember, when you were well, how beautiful you were, how alive? You'd chase after me to punish me for being naughty. Do you remember our house in Fez, the last house my father built?'

It was big and not very comfortable. In winter we'd freeze, we slept under heavy blankets, the floor was made of concrete. Father couldn't afford to buy terracotta tiles, let alone marble – my aunt's house was full of marble imported from Italy, and we thought it the height of luxury. When I was a boy, I found out there were poor people, a lot of poor people, and rich people, but my aunt's husband was rich because he worked so hard. I adored him. He was a kind man, a reserved man. He always used to slip me some money. He'd smile and say I mustn't tell my father – he'd have been furious – but I'd give it to my mother, who was pleased. One day she asked me to go with her to the medina, to the Souk D'hab, the gold market. She took out a handkerchief, she'd knotted some coins into it. She showed it to me and said: 'This is your money. I've kept it, and now you're going to buy me a present with your money.' A present! No one had ever given her one. Nothing, not even a bunch of flowers or a box of chocolates. My mother was proud and happy that her son was buying her her first present. I counted the money and said to the jeweller: 'What will you give me for this amount?' He counted the notes, then, looking at my mother, he said: 'That'll buy you a bangle! Choose the one you like – no, not the chunky one, take one of the thin ones, and besides, the chunky ones aren't in fashion any more.'

My mother dithered for ages, then made up her mind. She handed it to me and waited for me to present it to her. I felt emotional, and so did she.

'Do you remember? I've never forgotten the bangle story. Later I bought you your first gold belt. I remember the comment my aunt made; she thought hers more beautiful. "But times have changed," you answered, saying you didn't want such a heavy, expensive jewel, but you had accepted it to please your son. You wore it for a while, then one day you gave it to my wife.' My mother gives a wan smile, then groans. Smiling is painful. I squeeze her hand. She attempts to squeeze mine. After an hour by her bedside, I become used to her paleness and her tremendous fatigue. When I arrived the other day, it was a shock to see her. Hiding my face in my hands, I cried.

I went to the cemetery with my older brother. We had to make some plans. I laughed nervously. I told him jokes, to avoid thinking about what we were meant to be doing, which was choosing a site for our mother's grave. Laroussi, who was in charge of the cemetery, showed us several plots, expressing his sorrow all the while: 'May God deliver her. This would be a lovely spot, facing the town and, even better, the mountain. It's so green and the view is wonderful. She must be an important person who loves tranquillity and the blue of the sky. Unless you'd rather put her on the other side, but I wouldn't advise it, you'd have to walk over several graves to get to it. I don't recommend the white ones.

Here would be nice … Come, come and stand in the exact place. What do you see? You're admiring the landscape, it's beautiful, this side's very much in demand, the well-to-do reserve plots. I presume that money's no problem …'

We visit every inch of the cemetery. I stop trying to lighten the mood. A funeral procession goes by. Laroussi comments: 'It's midday, and that's the sixth burial today. Yesterday we had eleven dead. That's unusual. There are days without any. But that's just my cemetery, I don't know about the others.' Again and again we walk past my father's grave. My brother stops to say a prayer. I notice the grave is set back from the path. I ask Laroussi if there's room for another. He glances at it, then says: 'Thirty-five centimetres by one metre sixty. Let's see, yes, it's possible.'

I'm surprised. Thirty-five centimetres isn't much. Laroussi interrupts, informing me, as if I were an infidel: 'We Muslims bury our dead lying on their right sides, facing Mecca, not on their backs, like the Christians.'

So one day I too will be buried lying on my right side, my head turned towards Mecca. I picture my mother's tiny body all curled up on the right, and Mecca looking at it. I also think of my father, a believer often beset by doubts and anger. Was he a good Muslim? He said his prayers regularly, he blessed us and invoked Allah's goodness and mercy, he fasted, albeit resentfully, venting his temper on my mother or the young man that worked with him. But he wouldn't hear talk of the pilgrimage to Mecca. He loathed the Saudis, though he had no direct experience of them. Pilgrims would come and tell him about their misadventures in Mecca and complain about the conditions. In any case, he couldn't afford to carry out this duty of every Muslim. He said as much, citing a verse from the Qur'an.

In these early days of winter, a warm spring-like sun gives the cemetery a disconcerting light. The graves aren't in geometric rows. They jostle each another, as if the dead were about to sit down and admire, or beseech, the sky – the sky that's so sparing with rain. People actually staged a demonstration once calling for rain. They marched through the town, imploring God's mercy. Drought's an obsession in this country, and prayers are a sign of powerlessness. Laroussi asks if we've made up our minds. We look at one another without saying anything, then, as if to press us to come to a decision, he starts boasting about the view from this spot, forgetting that he's already done so: 'Look, the vista is superb. You have to think of the people who'll be coming to pray at her grave. It's better if they have a lovely view. Otherwise there's the other side, which looks out on the other cemetery. When people come to visit the dead, it would be better not to have other graves in the way.'

My brother tells him we've opted for the grave right next to my father's.

I venture a joke. 'I'm not sure they'd be thrilled to find themselves in the same bed again!'

Laroussi pretends he hasn't heard. My brother laughs. So do I. Laroussi begins to explain how he'll go about digging a twin grave with two headstones. He shows us a wide grave and says: 'Xdent!' He means road accident. A couple who died on impact, buried in the same grave.

When I get back to the house, I find my mother in terrible pain. It hurts her to be touched. I can sense how tired, how worn-out she is, and I start to pray, wishing she might be granted a gentle release. I know my brothers are thinking the same thing, but we don't speak. We exchange glances and each of us reads the same prayer on the faces of the others. My big brother tells me that Islam forbids euthanasia, but that there is a prayer to hasten deliverance. He cites the standard formula: 'To Allah we belong and to Him we shall return.'

She dozes, and from time to time calls out to her mother and her little brother. I reassure her, saying they're on their way. At no time does she utter her daughter's name. I'm not even sure she recognises me. I take her hand. Every mother recognises her child on touching their skin. Her arm and her hand are so thin I'm afraid I'll hurt her. She gazes at the ceiling and she's off. She falls asleep and now she's in Fez, playing hide-and-seek with her little brother. She calls his name, gives a little cry, then she drifts off. She's no longer here. I watch her breathing. She's not able to close her mouth. Her memories taunt her, they come and go, give her the illusion she's living and laughing, and then they cloud over and disappear into a well. She's afraid she'll be dragged in, she'll lose her footing and won't be able to climb out again. She's fighting with shadows. I see her hand move, as if trying to brush someone off. She can barely form words. We guess what she wants to tell us. Keltum can make out these half-spoken words easily. Does she recognise them or is she imagining them, acting from habit? She knows when to give her a drink, when to change her. My mother keeps trying to say something. We lean over her, in an effort to understand. She wants to go to the toilet. Keltum says: 'You can pee, there's no problem, I've just put a pad on you.' But my mother refuses to pee in the pads. She holds it in. It's impossible to carry her; the minute anyone touches her, she shrieks in pain.

The house is no longer my mother's house. Fortunately, she isn't able to see what's become of it – a sort of shelter, like the ones in slums. In the kitchen, dirty dishes are piled up next to the dirty linen. In the sitting room, damp is eating away at the mattresses. Only the bathroom is clean. There's no toilet paper. Disease and death are also evident in the little day-to-day things, the apparently trivial details, the neglect, the sadness imbuing the objects and the walls. Disease or death, which is the more intolerable? A friend who was battling a disease that was consuming his body once said to me: 'Death, true death, unbearable loss and absence, is the illness – the endless days and nights of decline, suffering and helplessness. That's what death is, not that fraction of a second when the heart stops.'

And so my mother is dying. As she would have said, were she able to speak: 'I'm collecting time and days, I bend over and pick them up in scraps. It's not much, just some fragments of passing time, it's not nothing. But if you're all here, I'll be able to stop stooping over this debris of time. I've had enough of storing up the empty hours, the whole days that blur with the nights, dreams that play tricks on me, memories that get bored and restless, like fish out of water. I'm drowning. I'm just going, and then a wave brings me back to the shore. I can't feel anything, but I'm all wet, I'm ashamed I can't dry myself. I'm losing control. What's the good of telling you I've had enough, it's all in God's hands? He's the one who guides my feet on this flat sea where I'm sinking and then pull myself up, it all depends on His will. I've forgotten to pray, I don't know where I am any more, I'm going, my eyes are half-shut, my mouth open. Oh, I hate this hole! Why can't I close my mouth? I'm snoring. I've always hated snoring, my last husband never worried about waking me up with his snoring. I can't control anything any more. I want to go to the bathroom. I refuse to wet myself, no, I'm holding my water in, my bladder hurts, but I won't give in. Not that! Not that! I'll call Keltum. She can't hear me, or is she pretending? I'm reaching out my hand, no one's beside me. Where are my children? I know they're here, this is when I need to feel them. They're talking in the next room. I can hear them. I feel better. I'll tell them to pray for me, to pray to God not to forget me.'

34

'When the power of speech goes, it means the end is near,' says my cousin, a good man. He adds: 'But everything's in God's hands! Who knows who'll be the first to go? So listen, I've already reserved a shroud for your mother. I had set it aside for myself, but I'm still hanging in there, and anyway, it is all in God's hands. Don't hesitate to call me, any time, day or night. I know there are practical matters to attend to, and you're still young – inexperienced in these things, I mean. But I make no assumptions – life, death, illness, old age, time, it all comes and goes with the wind and the storms. Do we have any choice? I manage as best I can with this old prostate, I force myself to go out and walk for a good hour every day, even though what I see makes me deeply unhappy. I'm very fond of your mother, she's the incarnation of grace, generosity and patience. She recognised me, you know, even though her tongue is heavy and she finds it hard to articulate her words. Just think, if we had old people's homes in Morocco! I'd be in one and so would your mother. How awful! How wicked! Right, I'm going on with my walk, and don't forget, I'm taking care of the shroud!'

My mother's finding it harder and harder to wake up. She sleeps very deeply. How can we wake her? Keltum complains; she must give her her medication. I simply watch. She is somewhere else, perhaps in another city, another life. She climbs mountains and comes back down, as light as air. She used to love that image: climbing up and down, to express her confusion, her dissatisfaction. Where is she now? She no longer talks about Fez or her old childhood home. When she was little, she didn't play with dolls, but with the vegetables her mother was preparing for lunch. She'd give each of them a name and a job, then she'd throw them into the pot, which irritated her mother. That was how she learned to cook.

'These are the consequences of lying supine,' the doctor tells me. Remaining horizontal creates all kinds of problems in her body. She calls out. I think it's a cry for help. No, she's worrying about dinner. Is the pot on the stove? That's what she wanted to say. Manning her post to the end. It's Keltum who translates her attempts at speech. She guesses, rather than hears, what my mother means.

I feed my mother. My mother, my child. A spoonful of milk and cheese. A little girl eating, her eyes closed, and my hand trembling with emotion. Tears well in my eyes. I give up. Keltum takes over and feeds her with a practised hand. I leave the room and wipe my eyes, thinking not of my mother, but of my children. I'm not sure how this transference occurred.

Taking her hand, feeling the bones under her withered skin, talking to her, telling her a story and waiting for her eyelids to twitch or her lips to move slightly. Memories need sunshine, light and music. It's summer on the terrace of the house in Marshan, overlooking the sea. The east wind is raging, which irritates my mother, and she says she wishes we still lived in Fez, in the medina, where the wind never ventured. I watch her and again I see her knotting a headscarf under her chin. She loved watching the sea with its little white waves, heralding the arrival of a wind said to drive people mad. In the hazy light of the past, voices mingle and eyes meet, searching out beauty and serenity. Mother's nature has always been serene. She's never completely lost her ability to be gracefully present in the world. Still today, that's what stands out. Perhaps the most upsetting thing is that her suffering undermines a grace that's always been entirely natural.

She smiles, and closes her eyes. She has no desire to see herself reduced to a sick child. Off she goes through the alleyways of Fez, and spends the whole afternoon at the Moulay Idriss mausoleum. She claims he's her ancestor, who came from Arabia in 808 and founded the town of Fez. She talks to him, confiding her worries, the burden of watching over her sick son and encouraging her other son to do well at school. 'Oh, Moulay Idriss, saint of saints, the man closest to Sidna Muhammad, our Prophet, hear my prayer. Don't forget me, keep illness from my door, make your light open the way to goodness. Oh, Moulay Idriss, our city's patron, virtuous man, be the messenger of my trust and my faith. Let my house fill with your light, give me a sign so that I can go on being healthy enough to look after my children, and my husband, who never has any luck. Keep the evil eye away from us – the eye of the envious, the jealous – the evil eye of all those that make their pact with Satan. I don't know the right response to the harm done me, I only know how to pray, I only know the path that leads me to you!'

No need for a go-between here. The bond is strong, it's part of her, as it was part of her mother and her grandmother. Every Thursday she'd ask my father's permission to go to Moulay Idriss. She'd set off with her cousin, her best friend, taking a little money, which she'd discreetly slip into the collection box at the mausoleum entrance. She'd give what she could and never mention it. By evening she'd be happy and radiant, no longer worried. The visit meant freedom. When she said her evening prayers, we heard her reminding Moulay Idriss of everything she'd told him. My father made no comment, but a surreptitious, mocking smile played on his lips.

Keltum's on edge. She cries a lot. The house is a shambles now. I think back to what my mother would say: repaint the walls, get the living room ready for the funeral. My cousin with the shroud calls me. He thinks that Keltum is profiting from the situation. 'Your mother's a fine lady, she deserves to have an end that's dignified, that has some class. But Keltum's an ignoramus, a village woman who wants us to feel she's indispensable. For a start, your mother needs to go back to her own room and her own bed. She's unhappy there, because the two women want to be in the room where the TV is. I realise she's in no state to be carried, but with two strong nurses I know, Layachi and Lamrani, we can take her to her room without hurting her. And too bad about the Egyptian or Brazilian soap opera! She's your mother, and it's your duty to ensure she's comfortable. You know, even if she can't speak, even if she no longer has the energy to make her wishes known, she knows when things aren't right. Talk to her, even if she seems not to hear you. On the contrary, she can hear you and she loves whatever you say. Her hearing's still good. Don't be taken in by appearances. Now, you're coming to the cemetery with me tomorrow. Laroussi has reserved some plots. I'll talk to him. A fine lady can't be buried next to the path, even if it is beside her husband. And I'm taking care of the shroud. Don't forget that. See you tomorrow.'

35

Insomnia. My mother's face fills the space. She's posing for Zaylachi, our photographer friend. She adjusts her headscarf, looks straight into the lens and attempts to smile. She's barely fifty. This is somewhere near the start of her health problems. She watches me. I'm standing behind Zaylachi. He says to me: 'My mother had the same thing. Sadly, she died while I was away studying in the USA.' He tells her about it. She answers with a prayer: 'May God take me in my children's lifetime!' Or: 'May God keep us from being separated!'

Again I think of Roland, who doesn't understand how close I am to my mother. He tells me: 'The interesting ties are those that can be broken or challenged. But you cling to your mother the way a lost soul clings to saintliness.' It's true – and so what? I love my mother for what she is, for what she's given me and because that love is near religious. I often ask myself what I would be without my parents' blessing. Blessing has nothing to do with religion. But we owe respect, support and love to those who made us. I'm not ashamed of asking for that blessing. It's a passion, a silk thread stretched between two beings. A love that's free, simple and obvious.

One summer's day in Fez, I saw a father publicly cursing one of his sons. He withdrew his blessing from him and asked God to refuse him His mercy. A crowd formed, everyone had something to say.

'A son cast out from his family is a lost man.'

'A son that's cursed will go straight to hell.'

'A father pushed to that extreme deserves our pity. But the son deserves to be isolated and scorned.'

'God will abandon him in Gehenna, eternal hell!'

She wanted to see the sea, smell the tang of seaweed, remember the time she lived in Marshan, facing the Strait. So she'd agreed to go and stay with her son for a few days. She wasn't very ill yet. Sometimes she'd go out, to visit Hassan the jeweller, then Drissia the dressmaker. That was twenty years ago. Her son's wife had left her at home while she went off to see her parents. In the late afternoon, my mother wanted her tea with milk, as usual. Everything had been locked, the cupboards, the drawers, even the door to the kitchen. When her son came home, he found her outside the door, in her djellaba, wailing: 'I want to go home now. I'm not wanted here. She locked everything before she left. No one's ever done such a thing to me, ever! The shame of it! To be invited to my son's house, then humiliated by his wife! Where are we? Who are we that we've sunk to this level of meanness? I only wanted some tea. My God, what's she afraid of, this ill-mannered girl? That I'd take her things? The shame, son! Go on, take me home right now. I won't drink tea for the rest of my life, because if I do, it will bring back memories that are too painful!'

Luckily, she's forgotten that incident. The house is heavy with silence. The sky is grey. Keltum is snoozing. She's thinking of the future. Maybe she'll refuse to leave the house; she's already demanding a share of the proceeds. The other woman's dreaming of a man, a husband, a family. The objects look sad. There's almost no crockery left. Everything gets broken. My mother kept her house like a small palace. But now, the place is in a woeful state.

June 1956. Tangier, international city. A city devoured by Europe, a city open to the world – so open it's considered a den of spies and bandits, a trafficking hub, but above all a city outside of time, that's turning its back on Morocco, on Moroccan traditions and customs. My mother felt as if she was on holiday there, but she missed Fez. The Spanish were the most numerous, and also the most active. They weren't seen as occupiers, they were almost as poor as us. The French and the British were arrogant, rich, powerful and contemptuous, they didn't like the Spanish, considered them as backward as the Moroccans. It was hard to gain

228

entry to their schools and lycées. There was a primary school opposite my uncle's house: a school for the sons of the elite. I asked my uncle who the elite were. He thought about it, then said: 'Definitely not you, or your cousins. We aren't distinguished enough to go to their schools, not rich enough, we don't love the Frenchies enough.' The Porte tea-rooms were French-owned, a place where ageing Englishwomen came for their five o'clock tea. The British had a dog cemetery. We found that funny, even shocking. So much love for mutts, it was beyond us! The Italians had a palace, a school and a restaurant – Casa Italia. The Spanish had a hospital, they'd take in everyone there; they had wonderful nuns who looked after patients and their families. They also had a school and a Francoist newspaper, *España*. My mother couldn't count in pesetas, she used rials. Just like me. She went to the market and bought everything she needed for a big party. She was happy. My brother and I passed our primary school matriculation. My father framed the certificates and sent out invitations. Two days and two nights' preparation. Our uncles and boy and girl cousins all came. Our Jewish neighbour, my father's friend, arrived bearing presents: a Parker pen each. I sneaked away and followed my brother, who had a date with a pretty Spanish girl at the beach. My mother wept. 'I've made everything for the party and you're going to the beach! The shame of it! What do I tell our guests? How am I supposed to explain that our children would rather eat a tuna sandwich at the beach than the *pastilla* I've spent two days preparing?' When we got home in the late afternoon, there were still people there. I was sunburnt and my brother had got into a fight with the Spanish girl's cousin. It was a bad day. In the evening, we did the washing up, to earn our forgiveness. Mother was asleep.

She's looking at us, even though we know she can no longer see. Her eyes, still glassy and vacant this morning, flicker, as if seeking to light on something. She looks at us and says nothing. My sister tells me: 'I'm unlucky, I've always been unlucky. Mother's going to die without speaking to me. Why this silence? I'm her daughter, for heaven's sake! Yes, her own daughter, even if I was brought up by my grandmother, who was such a mother to me that I called Mother my big sister. That's what it is, I'm the eldest daughter, but she prefers you boys. I have no luck. The only man who understood me is dead. I'm alone, horribly alone. Look, her lips are moving, she's trying to talk, to talk to me, but she can't form the words. Can any of you make out what she's saying? It's hot, she's hot. I'm fanning her, like I used to do in Fez, when the summer was so suffocating. On my wedding day, it rained. People tried to convince me that it was a good omen. She's going to die, that's for sure, it's written. I know that everything is written, even if I can't always accept that it's God who took my husband from me. It was a runaway lorry that took him. God forgive me, sometimes I lose my mind and say whatever comes into my head. I only feel good in Mecca. I've made the pilgrimage seven times, five with my husband. That holy place is soothing, even my blood sugar returns to normal, my headaches disappear, my heart is light. We should have taken our mother to Mecca. She'd have been happy, so happy. She hasn't had much joy in her life. But now it's too late. Maybe God's reserved a place for her in paradise. I remember when she used to cry a lot because her husband treated her badly. He wasn't violent, but he was verbally cruel. Look, she's moving. Maybe she's thirsty. She hasn't got the strength to talk. She refuses to eat. Like a baby that rejects its mother's breast. She's looking at us, as if begging us to stop making her eat.'

36

Her grimaces, her exhaustion, her still hands unnerve us. My sister looks at me, Keltum looks at my sister, and I watch my mother's breathing.

The sky is blue. It's cold. Keltum has muted the TV. A procession of images. A pretty woman, over made-up, is talking, tanks roll across the screen, a burial, the pretty presenter is back, then images of young men running and throwing stones.

I tell myself: 'The day is blue, and so is the season. The silence is blue. And death is stalking the house. Maybe blue ushers in grey, the bitter hue of winter.'

My sister cries silently. Tears run down her face but she doesn't wipe them away. She looks lost. She's no longer here. She's thinking about her husband, how loving he was, his unbearable absence. Her husband was goodness itself, someone you could rely on. Killed outright. My sister wishes she could have died with him. That's what love is. She's never spoken the word. They loved each other without ever needing to say it, they were simply there for one another.

My brother's the peacemaker. How does he manage it? He believes everything's negotiable. My mother didn't like making decisions: she let time do its work. My father was never afraid of saying what he thought of people, even if it caused ructions.

We're all gathered round her, all thinking the same thing. Her eyes are half-closed, her breathing's laboured. The smell of cooking reaches her room. The windows are kept closed, for fear she'll catch cold. My brother slides a tape into a radio-cassette player. An Egyptian intones the Qur'an. A discussion begins on the different ways of reciting it. The Moroccan style's apparently the least popular, the Egyptians are the champions. I feel uneasy. One of my brothers murmurs the verses the Egyptian's reciting. My sister's pleased: it reminds her of her visits to Mecca. Mother is in a deep sleep. Keltum's in a foul mood, as if our being there annoys her. I feel useless. My brother tells me he feels the same. We are helpless. If we stopped her medication, she'd go during the night. Go, and not come back. Fly off, give her hand to the angel watching over her, let herself be quietly, weightlessly borne away, regaining, perhaps, the grace and beauty of the old days. My mother's sixteen, playing hopscotch in the courtyard of the big house. Her father sees her and pulls her up short: 'You're not a child any more, you're a woman now!' Her mother adds: 'You're jumping about as if you were a little girl, but you're pregnant! I'm going to tell your husband. He won't like it.' My mother lets down her long black hair and covers her face with it. Perhaps she's ashamed. She stops skipping and joins her mother in the kitchen, humming to herself. She smiles and pretends to dance.

Her face has gradually lost its wrinkles, her skin's become smooth and sallow: her time is over. We know it's passed, it's taken off, leaving no trace. Within a few days, she's shed the years that weighed her body down. For a long time now, she's been walking towards the end. She used to say: 'Death is a right, a right we can neither be rid of nor change. Death is a fact, it's above us, within us, from birth. So what is dying? This right is practised on us and we accept it in silence.' She has accepted it serenely, without ever being angry, with no protest. What's the point of arguing, of talking about it, of wanting more than anything to be stronger than the inevitable?

Her face is a girl's, appeased by a dream, by a promise, by a soft, generous spring. Her face has given itself to death, an act of the ultimate private truth. Who would lie at this moment? Alive, she was incapable of lying. As the end approached, she was even more beautiful, because lying never came into it.

Her death was slow and free of anger. Her body slowly deserted her. When she still had the strength to speak, she wanted to be washed, and have her hair combed, twice a day; mindful of her appearance to the end. Anguish now left her in peace. She no longer fretted. She knew we were all there with her, all together, devastated. We talked to her and her lips moved, but no sound came from her mouth.

Now her face was ready to be given to the earth. She was fond of that expression. She'd say: 'He who's given his face to the earth is no longer to be pitied. It's those left behind who are to be pitied, the ones who will have to live without him.'

She once said to me: 'You know, Rabi'a died in childbirth. It's like a voice that's been interrupted by something external. When it's sudden, that's what it's like, a telephone call cut off – you call, and you call, and then you can't believe there's no one on the other end of the line.'

She wasn't afraid of her own death, but she couldn't bear the rituals surrounding other people's. It was a childlike fear, an unsoothed nightmare. A cry in the night, the smell of perfume and Arabian incense. A stiff, icy hand pulling her towards a precipice. Death is nothing. But everything that lurks around it is unbearable.

Soon I'll arrive at the house. I'll go down Impasse Ali Bey. I'll push open the gate, and then the door. I'll look for her face from afar, and won't see it. I'll go into her room, where she's at rest now, until morning. She didn't spend the night in the fridge. She died at home. I'll lean over and kiss her face, as I did four years ago, before I left. I'll cry, there'll be a flood of tears and I'll find it hard to stop them. I don't know if they help. It's other people's tears that make mine flow, it's catching. I've never been ashamed to cry. I'll cry to empty my heart and my mind. And then the real tears, the ones I fear, are the tears that will wake me later, months and years after this 4 February 2002.

There'll be stubborn, haunting, cruel dreams. I'll see her young and beautiful again. I'll see her, pregnant with me, in the heat of the Fez summer. I'll see her at Sidi Harazem, when I'm still a baby sucking at her breast. I'll see her in the Ifrane spring, at my aunt's house. She'll be glowing, happy and carefree. I'm expecting these dreams and I'll be sad when I wake up, because Mother won't be there. I'll be the unconsoled child, the one bored by school, who prefers the intimate world of women and afternoon parties at the house. I'll seek refuge in the basement, among the earthenware jars of provisions, and I'll jump out and give her a fright. I'll emerge, jubilant at having managed to scare her. I'll see her in the crowd and she won't recognise me. I'll wake with a start and cry out for help. I'll go out on the terrace of our first house in Tangier and stand beside her, gazing at the sea. I'll talk to her but she won't hear me. I'll tell her I miss her and she'll let the wind tangle her hair and cover her eyes. She won't try to resist the wind. She'll turn around and set off on a journey, with the wind.

Perhaps tonight her mother, her father, her brothers and her husbands will welcome her, saying: 'What's happened to your wrinkles? Where's your white hair gone? You come to us with all your teeth. You're beautiful, short as you are … You called out for us so often that we've come to welcome you. For years, you called out for Moulay Ali, Yemma, Lalla,

Sidi Hassan – you called out for us all the time. So here we are, all of us. The journey wasn't so bad – the journey, or the crossing. You've arrived in the middle of winter. At last we're going to sleep, to sleep for a long time, for all eternity. Come, come to us, sit down, have a rest. You'll see, here time goes in circles, sometimes it makes our heads spin. You don't like that. When you were little, you fell off a merry-go-round at the Jnane Sbil Garden in the public park. You saw stars, you were giddy for a few minutes. Here, there's no merry-go-round. But you'll see, you can feel time on the wind it whips up as it passes. We don't worry about time or the wind. Nothing can touch us any more. As long as people remember us, we are here. Anyway, it's the wind that tells us, lets us know about the things we've left behind.'

37

Summer in Fez. It's very hot. My mother's playing brides with Lalla Khadija, her cousin and friend. They're on the terrace, where they've set up a tent as a *dakhchoucha* – the bridal chamber – and hung sheets to create shade. My mother is the bride. She stands up straight, eyes not lowered but closed. She's put rouge on her cheeks and lips and Lalla Khadija's drawn a black beauty spot on her right cheek. Lalla Khadija is playing the bridegroom and has given herself a beard and moustache with a piece of charcoal. As the man coming to fetch the bride who has been chosen for him, she arrives on horseback, acts out the scene, makes some noise, gives orders. My mother lowers the veil over her face. She's embarrassed and wants to laugh, especially when she realises that her cousin's taking her role seriously and the horse is just a reed. 'Come, follow me, mount this horse. You're my wife, you are mine. I hope your parents have taught you good manners, otherwise I will!' My mother doesn't reply. 'That's a good sign,' says Lalla Khadija, 'a young bride who holds her tongue, a pearl that obeys and does not protest, this is the woman I have chosen! You are well brought-up, and you come from a prominent, respectable family.' My mother lowers her head, then dissolves into fits of giggles, as does Lalla Khadija. She flings the *dakhchoucha* up in the air and shouts: 'We'll get married on the same day! I hope our parents choose two tall, handsome brothers for us. We'll be together. We'll always be friends.'

It's getting hotter and hotter. Lalla Khadija fills a bucket with water and pours it over my mother, who streaks across the terrace, picks up a bowl and splashes cold water over her cousin in retaliation. They laugh, slither, fall over, get up again and run, all thoughts of marriage banished. They are happy. They're barely eight years old.

The house. The house at the end of the cul-de-sac. The old house with its two withered shrubs, its wild grass that conceals a few empty pill packets discarded by Keltum or Rhimou. As if they lived in a slum, or a village. The old house with its thick, cracked walls, its windows that don't close properly, its damp mingled with cooking aromas, its frayed carpets and its two refrigerators, one of which hasn't worked in twenty years. The cooker black with grime, the poorly laid floor tiles in the bathroom, the two toilets in a sorry state, and so much dust gathered behind the chest of drawers. And the famous, supposedly Venetian mirror that fell off the wall of its own accord the night that death entered the living room. It fell but didn't shatter. My brother saw that as a sign from fate, a strange coincidence. My sister, who's superstitious, covered it with a sheet, saying that death cannot bear the presence of mirrors, because death must not be visible, betrayed by the reflection the looking glass might send back. But I saw death – through carelessness, and bad luck. I've seen my mother as I ought never to have seen her. The corpse-washer hadn't finished: her body lay on a plank. And there was her mouth, a gaping, round, black hole, a hole opening onto endless darkness, her hair plastered in black henna. Death is that hole, that black circle in a small head and that plank of new wood in the bedroom that used to be mine, more than twenty years ago. Death is that acrid, acid, burning gust that invades your lungs and heart, that smell of incense and damp, and the door that's closed on the body that's no longer my mother, which was ravaged by pain and has lost its breath, its soul. But where is my mother? That black hole is not her mouth, that little round head is not her head, that plank is not her bed.

Very quickly, absence, an immense absence, fills the house. The furniture and all the household things have become useless, old, battered, ugly. The mattresses, the cushions, the bow-legged table, the plates, the plastic chair, the wheelchair, the crutches, the stainless-steel cutlery, the ugly gilded glasses for tea, the television and its dangling aerial, the two hideous chandeliers in the living room, the napkins and the dozens of rags that Rhimou used for cleaning.

Keltum and Rhimou have gathered their belongings. Several suitcases and large hold-alls. They've helped themselves to anything they could carry, without asking, with no scruples. I don't care. But I don't like greed. Rhimou seems more human, more affected by this vast absence. Keltum says nothing. She goes from room to room, tries to appear grief-stricken, but her eyes dart everywhere. What else is there to take? Ah! The TV. But it's heavy. It's an old set, one of her sons will come and pick it up, unless one of the family wants it. She waits, tidies things, empties, comes and goes like a decapitated viper. She's not happy, she's anxious, that much is clear. The last act hasn't played out as she'd imagined. Things have gone wrong – strange things, like that suitcase full of caftans never worn by my mother that's disappeared, as has the Chinese tea service. Nothing's been said, as nothing was ever said: we all want this chapter, this ordeal, to be over. Keltum's about to leave. Rhimou is ready. She comes to say goodbye. I give her an envelope containing a voucher that can be exchanged for an airline ticket to Mecca. She's happy, she leaves in tears. Keltum watches the scene, then says: 'We need to talk.' Her tone is coarse, crude, inappropriate. She holds out her hand for her envelope, then withdraws it, repeating: 'We need to talk.' Her tone's nasty, downright threatening. My sister's crying because she couldn't find any of my mother's dresses. The thieving has gone on for years. My mother used to tell me: 'I keep one eye shut and the other open, but I prefer to say nothing. I'm afraid she'll leave me, she's quite capable of it. She's helped herself as she pleased, with no shame.'

Keltum wants more than a farewell present. What is she claiming, exactly? The house? The look in her eyes isn't encouraging. It's never been kind. Is she grieving? Someone says: 'Yes, she's grieving because the source of her income has dried up.' I daren't think about that ... She's in a filthy mood, a kind of rage, her eyes are dry, her presence bulky, her anger suppressed because it's the end of something. I close my eyes and thank her for all she has done over the years. She tells me that God is her judge and witness. She takes her envelope, opens it, turns her back to us to count the notes, then says: 'With this, I'll be able to go to Mecca too.'

I don't know if it's grief or the wind that raises the dust of memories and drenches them in bitterness. A painful furrow is dug, in the memory and in the heart. Bereavement disturbs the stones gathered by kids, and arranges them around the grave. The silence of petrified glances casts grey earth onto black, dug by the grave-digger's pickaxe. Back at the house, the emptiness is suffocating. We lock the shutters and doors as if about to set off on a journey. The house has been sealed by an irreparable absence. It no longer exists. I will never go back there. Nor will I go to her grave. It's not my mother who's underground. My mother is here, I can hear her laughing and praying, insisting the table be laid, that we eat the meal she's spent hours cooking. She's on her feet, delighted to see us all together, eating our favourite foods. She waits to be complimented. We happily devour everything but say nothing to her. Then she says: 'The plates are clean, there's the proof you liked what I made.' My eldest brother says to her: 'God grant you health and keep you for us, for ever, present and happy in our love.' And, smiling, we say: 'Amen'.

Tangier, August 2001–May 2007

Glossary

adul	A religious man certified by the government to draw up marriage certificates
Al-Fatiha	The opening surah of the Qur'an
babouches	Leather slippers
cherbil	Fine slippers worn by a bride
Cherif (pl. Chorfa)	Descendant(s) of the Prophet Muhammad
dakhchoucha	Bridal chamber
djabador	Tunic
djellaba	Long, hooded cloak often made of wool
Eid al-Adha	The Festival of Sacrifice, also known as the Greater Eid, the second most important festival in the Muslim calendar. This festival remembers the prophet Ibrahim's willingness to sacrifice his son when God ordered him to.
Eid al-Fitr	Festival of Breaking of the Fast: this marks the end of Ramadan
Fassi	From Fez
fouta	Towel

gazelle	Used in Morocco to mean a woman who is sublimely beautiful and gentle, and hence for any beautiful woman
Haj/Hajja	Precedes the name of someone who has made the pilgrimage to Mecca
hajama	Barber who acts as a waiter at the wedding feast
hammam	Turkish bath
h'boura	Unsold, unwanted goods
Hizb al-islah al-watani	Party of National Reform
Istiqlal	Freedom (a political party)
kanoun	Potbellied terracotta barbecue
khli	Dried meat
kissaria	Covered market in the heart of the medina
Lalla	A title of respect when addressing a woman
mansouria	Long dress
mellah	Jewish quarter
mrouzia	A sweet and spicy lamb tagine traditionally prepared in the days following Eid Al Adha
M'sid	Traditional Qu'ranic school
negafa (pl. *negafates*)	Woman who oversees wedding celebrations
pastilla	A sweet-and-sour pigeon pie, emblematic of Fassi cuisine and Moroccan cuisine in general.
polished stone	Dry ablutions may be performed in place of washing if no clean water is readily available or if a person is ill, according to the Qu'ran
rasul	A natural mineral clay, mined in the Atlas Mountains of Morocco since the eighth century. It is combined with water to form a sticky unguent for washing the body and has been used by Moroccan women for centuries in caring for their skin and hair.

Razzaq	The name Razzaq means 'servant of the all-providing'
sadaquah	Alms is the concept of voluntary giving in Islam. The term stems from the Arabic root word *sidq*, which means sincerity. So giving *sadaqah* is considered a sign of sincere faith.
sbohi	After the wedding, the bride spends the night at her new husband's for the first time. The next day, she has her first breakfast with her new family, and her own family joins them in the morning with traditional cakes for the festivities.
seroual	Baggy trousers, for man or woman
Sharia	Islamic law
Si/Sidi	Lord/master. Si is a variant.
surah	Chapter or section of the Qur'an
tagine	North African stew of meat and/or vegetables
taqbib	Washing with buckets
tarbouche	Man's cap, typically of red felt, with a tassel at the top
tayaba (pl. *tayabates*)	Bath attendant / masseuse at the hammam
tbak	Decorated basket
tchamir	Long, thin chemise
tolba	Men learned in the Qur'an who chant Qur'anic passages at funerals.
Yemma	Mother in Kabyle
Zakat	Purifying alms. A certain amount of money or property is collected from those who are wealthy and given to the poor.